BEST OF FRIENDS

BEST OF FRIENDS

•

Jilliene McKinstry

AVALON BOOKS
NEW YORK

Published by Thomas Bouregy & Co., Inc.
160 Madison Avenue, New York, NY 10016

Library of Congress Cataloging-in-Publication Data

McKinstry, Jilliene.
   Best of friends / Jilliene McKinstry.
      p. cm.
   ISBN 0-8034-9762-8 (alk. paper)
   I. Title.

   PS3613.C566B47 2006
   813'.6—dc22   2005033810

PRINTED IN THE UNITED STATES OF AMERICA
ON ACID-FREE PAPER
BY HADDON CRAFTSMEN, BLOOMSBURG, PENNSYLVANIA

To Samantha, for inspiration, for the laughter,
fairy tales, and cat stories.

FIC
329-8224

Prologue

The floor squeaked under Devon's foot as she tiptoed toward the door. She stopped, holding her breath, waiting to be discovered. She counted to ten, but not a sound came from the cabin as her parents and the boys continued sleeping. She carefully slid the door open, then closed it without a sound. Still holding her breath, she crept down the steps and walked down the path toward the boat dock. She carried a flashlight, something no six-year-old should be without on a late-night adventure. She didn't dare turn it on though, for fear it might scare her prey.

As she reached the end of the dock, she sat down, wrapping herself into a tight ball to wait and wonder how long before she would see them. Maybe she wouldn't be able to see them, she thought, for a moment worried. Maybe water fairies were invisible. She had forgotten to ask Pat about it earlier.

Devon shivered in the darkness trying to imagine what the magical fairies might look like. The idea captured her every thought since that afternoon. She had been sitting in this very spot, watching the river, when she asked her father, "Where does all the water go?" He had given her some baffling explanation about cumulo-something clouds and evap-something-rations and oceans and mountains and valleys. She sat there, her face screwed into a mask of concentration while she tried to fathom his tale, then tried again, "But where does the water *go?*"

Pat had finally told her the truth. "The water fairies take it," he said. Then he explained that the water fairies came quietly each night and carried all the water back up the hills so that the river never ran out.

Devon wondered why her father couldn't have explained it so simply, but then it was like that with Pat. His father and hers were best friends, and had been since the dinosaurs lived, according to Devon's mother. So Devon and Pat had known each other forever. He was like a big brother to her and she loved him dearly. Being a much older and wiser sixth-grader, he had good answers for most of her questions and the ones he didn't, he told her to ask her mother. Even her mother liked Pat's explanation about the water fairies more than the ridiculous thought of water disappearing into the clouds. Everyone knew clouds couldn't hold water!

Devon nearly fell in the river when the dock creaked

behind her. Whirling around, she gripped her flashlight tighter, then sighed in relief. "You scared me to death," she whispered as Pat knelt next to her.

"Sorry," he whispered back. "Thought you might like some company."

She scooted over, making room for him. They sat together, watching the water bubble and gurgle along. Silently wishing she had remembered to bring a warm sweater, Devon snuggled closer to Pat until he pulled his sweatshirt off and handed it to her. She tugged it on, pulling the soft material over her legs, then slipped a small hand into his larger one and sat waiting.

Every now and then Pat pointed to a bit of silver flashing on the river. "There! Did you see her?" Devon thought she did, but the fairies were so fast, it was hard to be sure. They watched for a long time, listening to the happy sound of the water dancing. It sounded so pretty and the sweatshirt was so warm. Devon yawned and tried to keep her eyes open. She leaned a little more into Pat's side and then relaxed completely as the water fairies continued to playfully steal the water for another day. The next morning she woke in her own bed, still in Pat's sweatshirt and secure in the knowledge she had seen the water fairies hard at work.

Chapter One

Twenty-two years later

The Rosemary mansion looked like it might have in its heyday some eighty years earlier, but then it would have been truly elegant and sophisticated. Not like the dilapidated but historical monolith it had become. For just this one night, the mansion had been rescued by a fairy godmother named Devon Kelly. The crystal chandeliers sparkled a rainbow of colors onto the ornately sculpted ceiling. The water fountains bubbled cheerfully in the ballroom as guests at the Eugene Historical Society ball enjoyed themselves. A string octet played Vivaldi's Concerto Number Two in G minor, complemented by the delicate chimes of champagne flutes clinking.

Devon looked about the festivities and knew the oak-paneled walls had not seen this much velvet and satin in decades. It was her job to change that. As Director of the Historical Society, she was responsible for saving the mansion built by one of the town's earliest millionaires.

Tonight's ball would be a chance for people to see the beauty of the hardwood floors and the charming and delicate Italian wall lamps. With any luck the guests wouldn't notice that the plumbing was leaking like the Titanic and many of the fine etchings on the ceiling were really just cracks. If she were lucky, the walls would remain intact until after midnight. Then the grand mansion could turn back into a pumpkin. The building would have to be carefully gutted anyway if they hoped to preserve it.

In the meantime, the women were beautiful, the men were handsome, and the tickets cost a fortune so everyone was enjoying the "free" champagne immensely. Devon knew the evening would be a success if people considered it a chance to see and be seen. Heads turned all over the ballroom, spotting this local business leader or that university coach. But of all the recognizable faces, none of them garnered as much attention as the tall, dark-haired man standing to her right.

Devon supposed with some amusement that he was handsome and well-dressed. His tall, broad shoulders filled out the tuxedo with superb lines. He stood in their circle of friends and joined their easy banter, an attractive smile lighting his features now and again. But she knew it wasn't his looks or even his position in one of Eugene's leading families that had so many women glancing his way. It was The Curse. The McKenzie Man Curse.

It was a powerful thing, this curse. It was renowned as being sudden and terminal. Every man picked as the city's most eligible bachelor by *McKenzie Magazine* publisher Eugenia Barstow had fallen to the curse. It always had the same result—an immediate case of sweating palms, followed by loss of attention and then mild heart palpitations. The ending was predictable for its victim. Within weeks he would develop a terminal case of matrimony. It never failed. Eugenia would pick the most witty, most handsome, most engaging man around and wham! He'd be white-faced and standing at the alter within weeks with a look of dismay as though he wasn't quite sure how he had gotten there. Until now.

Patrick Lawrence, the latest man saddled with the dubious honor, appeared ready to break the curse. It had been six months and he suffered no unsightly side affects. His vision was still clear, if somewhat bemused by the notoriety. It was a miracle he still saw women in the same calm, gentle manner he had always viewed them. In six months he had suffered late night phone calls, e-mails that could make a sailor blush, and phone numbers slipped into the oddest places.

In spite of the sometimes insane behavior of those around him, his hands were steady, whether presenting closing arguments in a trial or casting his fishing pole. Somehow he survived unscathed. According to the bachelor men in the ballroom, it was a miracle. It was a tragedy to some of the women.

Within their circle of friends, the curse was also an unending source of conversation. Mitch Broderick was perhaps the most relieved when Pat was chosen as the McKenzie Man. Now, he was the most amused by the mayhem. "Any strange and bizarre curse moments today?" he asked Pat.

Pat gave his friend a disgusted look. "Define strange. And speaking of bizarre, Sunny said to check your e-mail for those meeting notes."

"Isn't your new assistant working out?" Mitch asked in an overly innocent voice.

"New assistant? What happened to Margaret?" Devon asked.

"Margaret is taking a month off to visit her grandson in Alaska," Pat explained.

"How did you manage that?" Devon asked, knowing Pat's faithful executive assistant never took a vacation. Margaret had been with him since he began working for the city of Eugene after law school and as far as anyone could remember, she had never taken more than a couple of days off for herself.

Pat shrugged. "She just decided it was time."

"With a little arm twisting," Mitch added.

"What did you do?" Devon asked, arching an eyebrow at her best friend.

"I reminded her she had worked for me for eight years without taking a real vacation," Pat said in a calm, even tone.

"And?" she prompted.

"And that if she ever wanted me to run for public office she needed to take one," Pat told her with a perfectly straight face.

"Excuse me?" Devon asked, being fairly certain Pat had no intention of ever entering politics.

"Well, I told her if I ever ran for president they would investigate my employees and think of the scandal if anyone found out I never let my assistant go visit her grandson." Devon laughed at his ingenuity. Margaret would walk on hot coals for Pat and he knew it.

Dan Lawrence looked at his older brother in disbelief. "And she fell for it? I find that hard to believe. Margaret has never believed any of my tales over the years."

"That's because I don't tell her *tales*," Pat told him in the condescending voice that came with a lifetime of big-brother seniority.

Mitch snorted. "No, you just used the most amazing case of emotional blackmail I've ever seen."

Pat shrugged. "It seemed like a good idea and it was for a good cause." Then he grimaced. "So Margaret is up watching the whales and I'm trying to survive without her."

"So, who's your new assistant?" Devon asked.

"Mitch loaned me his administrative assistant from the planning department." Pat gave his friend a chilling look while Mitch tried unsuccessfully to keep a straight face. "Only five days and I'm ready to set sail for Anchorage," Pat muttered.

"Is she incompetent?" Dan asked.

"No, she's competent enough," Mitch answered. "And prompt and extremely professional."

"And persistent," Pat finished. "The most persistent woman I've ever seen. Next to you, of course," he told Devon.

"Isn't that a good thing?" Devon retorted.

"Not when you're the McKenzie Man," Mitch laughed, saluting Pat with his crystal glass. There were several collective "ahs" from the other friends in their circle.

Devon shook her head in sympathy. If she was female and she was persistent it could only mean one thing. Pat was in hot retreat from another ardent admirer.

Devon couldn't resist. "I take it she's enamored with the curse."

"Yep," Mitch said cheerfully. "She's downright dogged about it, too. Seems to think it will reflect badly on all women if he gets away."

Devon shook her head. "Poor Pat," she said, also trying to keep a straight face. "It must be terrible to have every eligible woman within fifty miles after you." Pat shot her a warning look that didn't dampen her amusement one bit. Personally, Devon couldn't see what the big deal was. Most people, even men, thought the curse was hilarious, unless *they* were its next victim.

In the beginning it had been amusing that the nominee would fall in love shortly after and marry, but now it had gone beyond coincidence. Now, confirmed bachelors all over the Willamette Valley cringed when the magazine announced it had a new victim. Then the relieved sighs followed as each realized he had been spared. For the victim, the nightmare was only beginning. Soon the swarms of women fascinated as much by the curse as the man would take notice and in a matter of weeks the poor man's carefree bachelorhood would be history, doomed to the wedding march. It was rumored the previous nominee pleaded with Eugenia to chose someone else, anyone else, but to no avail. When Eugenia chose a victim, she was determined.

"What are you going to do?" Devon asked Pat.

"I'll never hear the end of it if I send her back. She really is competent."

"Why don't you ask her out?" Dan, who had been suspiciously quiet, asked.

"Excuse me?" Pat returned. "Have you lost your mind?"

"I'm serious," Dan told him. "Do something together that you really love. Maybe she'll figure out that you're not meant for each other."

Pat frowned as he considered the drawbacks. There had to be serious ones if Dan had come up with the idea. "I don't date women in my office," Pat told him.

"She's not really from your office," Dan reminded him. "Maybe she's the right woman and you just need some time together."

Devon watched this interchange with some interest, wondering what Dan was up to. She couldn't believe he was really serious about giving Pat romantic advice. Dan's history with women looked like a long road trip of drive-through restaurants. Fast, low-maintenance, and on the move.

Pat's eyes narrowed as he looked at his younger brother. "You mean take her out to dinner?" he asked. "How will that discourage her?"

"I wasn't thinking of eating dinner. How about catching it?" Dan said.

A blank look crossed Pat's face while Devon grasped Dan's plan. "That's it," she agreed. "Take her fishing."

Dan nodded at her. "You could leave Friday night, go to the cabin, and by Saturday afternoon she'll want to go home."

"What if she likes it?" Pat asked, still unconvinced.

Mitch's date, Elise, rolled her eyes. "No woman likes spending a romantic weekend with a bunch of smelly fish."

"Devon does," Pat said honestly.

"Yes, she does," Dan said thoughtfully. "That's why she's coming, too."

"What?" Devon exclaimed.

"You and I can come along as chaperones—or witnesses." Dan gave his older brother a grin. "It's the least we can do. After all," he turned to Devon, "you were the one who mentioned Pat to Eugenia and got him in all this trouble."

Devon flushed pink with guilt. She interfered because Pat mentioned their friends who were happily married and that perhaps it was time to settle down. She thought she was being helpful. Instead, all he had developed was a severe aversion to aggressive women. Pat looked to her for help. She shrugged. "I don't see what it could hurt."

Pat groaned. "Famous last words."

Chapter Two

"That's the last of it," Devon said as Dan closed the Jeep's tailgate.

"It better be. I'll have to rent a U-Haul if you bring anything else," Dan said under his breath.

"Excuse me, but when you realize you've forgotten everything you need, I'll be the one you come running to," Devon told him as she snapped on her seatbelt.

"Yeah, like I'm going to need a propane fuel curling iron," he told her with a grin. "I thought you were bad in high school. Remember that time we went to the coast on Christmas break and you packed four bags for three days? You've just gotten worse with age."

Devon stuck her tongue out at her old friend and plumped her pillow. They bantered back and forth during the forty-minute drive along the McKenzie River to the cabin the Lawrence and Kelly families had shared for thirty years. Devon relaxed against the headrest and thought about the history she had with these Lawrence men. Her relationship with Dan sometimes looked more like sibling rivalry as they had survived their share of squabbles over the years, including the time Dan pushed her off a swing in first grade and broke her arm.

Pat, after threatening to strangle his little brother, carried her home, then held her while her mother took her to the emergency room. He hadn't even teased her when she cried, even though she made sure Dan was out of sight before she allowed herself the luxury. The pattern continued throughout their lives. Dan and Devon scrapping like brother and sister, with Pat offering the steady shoulder for her to cry on. Devon sighed as they continued up the winding, two-lane highway along the scenic river.

"Penny for your thoughts," Dan offered.

"I was just thinking about when Pat gets married. Things won't be the same."

Dan was quiet for a moment. "Maybe the curse won't take with him."

"I don't think he's going to be a bachelor forever, curse or not."

"No, I suppose not," he agreed. "I'm surprised it's taken this long. Pat was the one guy I know who didn't freak out about being the McKenzie Man."

"Except when it comes to locker rooms," she said with a grin. They both laughed over the incident a month ago when a determined grandmother had been so busy telling Pat about her precious granddaughter that she hadn't noticed they had entered the men's locker room at the Eugene Club. It was a toss-up as to who was more embarrassed, the little old lady or Pat. "And now assistants," she added.

Dan spared a sideways glance at her. "What if Pat is wrong?"

"What do you mean?"

"What if she is right for him?" he asked.

Devon shook her head. "I'd think he would know if the right woman was under his nose all this time."

"Hmm." Dan tapped his fingertips on the steering wheel thoughtfully. "Maybe they just need the right atmosphere," he said softly, almost as though to himself.

Devon looked at the scenery going by. The road climbed the foothills of the Cascade Mountains, following the McKenzie River upstream. As the river tumbled down the mountainside, blue water bubbled to white as it rumbled along through narrow canyons. Then it would mind its manners, gently sweeping through an occasional valley where houses and animals nestled near its beauty. Majestic Douglas fir trees formed the backdrop for maple, alder, and cottonwood stands, giving the river a wilderness setting. Stickery clumps of blackberry bushes, intermingled with fern and wild azaleas, crouched along the banks. Rhododendrons, their blooms long faded, rested now in shady green splendor, preparing to add bright splashes of color next spring.

If she were going to pick a place to fall in love, this would be it, Devon thought. There was something about this river that always called to her. The McKenzie wasn't as mighty or as well-known as the Willamette River, but it was still her favorite. The river was like a woman in her temperament—life-giving and powerful, serene yet volatile. It suited Devon perfectly and many of her happiest memories were here. The road dipped and turned a corner and there was the turnoff for the cabin. Devon wondered at the sudden lurch in her stomach as they pulled in beside Pat's SUV. A funny feeling of discomfort swept through Devon's being, forcing her to deeply inhale the mountain air. It must be that granola bar she ate for lunch.

"Everything okay?" Dan asked.

"Yeah, fine. Guess I should have eaten lunch," she told him as they walked to the front door.

Their fathers had purchased the one-story hunting cabin years ago. Moss covered the shake roof in soft, furry clumps and the wood siding had worn to a comfortable shade of grayish brown. Blackberry bushes on the south side crept near the walls as they did each summer and ferns sprouted wildly under the trees. They didn't see anyone as Dan bounded up the stairs. The steps creaked in a familiar tune while he called, "Hello? Anybody home?"

"Back here," a voice answered.

A huge yellow ball came loping around the cabin and launched at Devon. "Hello, Dorky," Devon knelt and hugged Pat's dog. The golden retriever then leaped around in circles, ecstatic to see her. "Where's your owner?" Devon asked, rubbing the dog's ears when she stood still long enough. With a happy bark the dog raced around the cabin toward the river. Dan wiggled his eyebrows at Devon as they followed, wondering what they would find.

Perched on a slight knoll looking down on the river, the cabin had been saved more than once from flood waters and the sloping lot gave it a treehouse feel. A wide porch ran across the back that was the site of countless sleep-outs and card games in their youth. Several chairs, a table, and a firewood bin crowded the rustic porch but there was no sign of Pat. Dan looked around and pointed to the river where two figures stood.

"You finally made it," Pat said with undisguised relief as they joined him on the short dock. Devon nearly laughed at the harried look on his face. Turning to the cause of his concern, she stopped, the smile freezing on her face. Standing before her was a strikingly beautiful woman who seemed just as surprised to see Devon.

"Devon, Dan, this is Sunny. She's been filling in for Margaret this week," Pat said, making the introductions.

"Nice to meet you," Dan said, giving Sunny his most flattering smile.

Devon shook her head in disgust. His older brother might not be interested, but Dan was obviously appreciating the view. Devon mumbled some appropriate greeting as she took in the golden hair cut in one of those perfect styles that never looked mussed. A short T-shirt and belted shorts showed off an exquisite figure.

Sunny looked like a fashion model posing in some wilderness location for a photography assignment.

"I was just telling Sunny how much I love it here," Pat told them.

"I can see why," Sunny said, wrapping a hand through Pat's arm. "It's beautiful here."

"Oh it's great, if you don't mind the mosquitoes," Devon told her cheerfully.

The dog trotted to Devon with a dripping stick, eager to play. Devon tossed it into the river for her, delighting the retriever. The beautiful blond gave Devon a thoughtful look. She glanced between Dan and Devon, then quirked a curious eyebrow at them. Devon flushed and wondered how to set her straight, then decided it didn't matter. They were here to disengage this woman from Pat's life. What Sunny thought of Devon's place in the picture was irrelevant. Devon arched an eyebrow back and decided to let her wonder. Sunny's eyes flared momentarily in surprise at the unspoken challenge, then she smiled. Devon smiled as well. It was going to be a very interesting weekend.

"I hope you didn't eat," Pat said. "I've got the grill ready."

"Great! I'm starved," Dan rubbed his hands together.

"So what else is new?" Devon teased as they moved to the porch. She left the men arguing over the grill and went inside to survey the kitchen. Someone had started a tossed salad and several ears of sweet corn sat ready to cook. Devon found a loaf of French bread and sliced it, adding butter and garlic salt.

"So how long have you and Pat known each other?"

Devon nearly jumped at the sultry voice from behind her. "All my life. Our fathers started a law firm together years ago."

"Who's your father?"

"Michael Kelly."

"Really? The judge?" Sunny asked. Devon nodded. "Hang 'em high Kelly," Sunny added almost to herself. "He's quite famous for his courtroom decisions."

"He calls them like he sees them," Devon said with a great deal of pride. "That's what a Superior Court judge is supposed to do."

"Hmm." Sunny carelessly twirled a wine glass with her red-tipped fingers. "Are you an attorney?"

"I'm an architect. I work on saving historical buildings."

"How interesting." Sunny made it sound as much fun as digging for potatoes. "I think Pat is wonderful. His work on the Jefferson case was simply breathtaking."

Devon frowned. That case had labored on for months and *it* seemed about as intriguing as dirt but she wasn't about to be outdone. "I was really proud of his work on the youth center."

"Oh yes," Sunny purred. "That poor little, grubby center. Personally, I could understand the business people wanting it removed. It really brought down the whole neighborhood having all those kids around."

Devon nearly sliced off a finger with the knife before she began mentally counting backward to calm herself down. Dan entered the kitchen, took one look at

Devon's expression and quickly retreated with the garlic bread. "So what do you think of the cabin?" Devon asked as she put the corn in the boiling water.

Sunny leaned one hip against the counter and seemed to consider. Devon wondered if the question was too difficult as the woman studied her carefully. "I suppose it's okay if you're the mountain-woman type." She examined a perfectly manicured nail. "Personally I prefer something a little more civilized."

Well, at least that part of Dan's plan seemed to be working, Devon thought. A few more hours of barbaric wilderness and Sunny and her manicure would be a streak out the door. As for this unpleasant woman being the right one for Pat, Dan had obviously lost his mind. Devon's spirits lifted considerably.

"So how long have you and baby brother been an item?" Sunny asked.

"We aren't an item. We are just old friends."

"Like you and Pat?" Sunny responded.

Somehow she made it sound like they had been caught playing post office as children. Devon opened the jar of sun tea and fought the unreasonable urge to dump it over the perfect coiffure. "No. Just friends. Some women can be just friends with men."

She realized that nasty arrow found its mark when Sunny's eyes narrowed. Devon felt the heat creeping up her cheeks. She had always prided herself on avoiding cat-fights but something about this woman definitely rubbed her the wrong way. Maybe it was that she was standing on hallowed ground here at the cabin, but

Devon had a fleeting suspicion that Sunny was intentionally rubbing her the wrong way.

"Only if they aren't smart enough to realize what a catch someone like Pat is," Sunny assured her. "What a waste that would be."

Pat popped his head in the door at that moment. "Everything okay in here?" he asked.

"Fine," Devon gritted out, giving him a black look.

"Good," he mumbled as he bolted from the kitchen as well.

Devon handed Sunny the tumblers filled with ice. "These need to go outside," she told her stiffly.

Their exquisite guest sauntered out the door, trailing a heavy scent of magnolias behind. Devon shook her head. Pat was right. This woman was the worst of his ardent admirers. With any luck she'd drown tomorrow while they were fishing and he wouldn't have to guard his honor anymore. Devon smiled suddenly at the thought of the six-foot-two Pat in hot retreat from the leggy beauty. Devon would bet her next check the barracuda in shorts would find Dan more her speed before the weekend was over.

That thought didn't bother Devon at all. Dan could handle his own woman problems. He had since second grade when Tracy Shears tied him to a tree with a jump rope at recess to steal a kiss. He charmingly convinced the teacher it was all his fault and then broke Tracy's heart when he offered the rope to an "older woman" third-grader.

These Lawrence brothers were so different in per-

sonality and physical traits that even their parents wondered at the difference sometimes. Dan was shorter by
an inch and built on a heavier frame of muscle, and his
golden brown hair took after their father, while Pat's
dark hair resembled their mother. In temperament they
were opposing poles of the same magnet as well. Dan
was more headstrong, outgoing, and likely to land up to
his ears in trouble as a youth. Pat was steady, calm, and
more likely to bail out his little brother.

"Hey! Where's the corn?" Dan called as Devon
picked up the bowl.

Devon chuckled. Female shark or not, Dan would be
able to handle her, no problem.

"That was great," Dan said as he pushed himself
back from the patio table. "What's for dessert?"

Devon pulled a face at him. "Aren't you ever full,
chowhound?"

Pat kicked his chair back and crossed his ankles
casually. "You're forgetting he's just a growing boy,
Dev," he teased.

"Then what's your excuse for seconds, old-timer?"
Dan asked as he wrapped his hands behind his head.
"At your age you should start watching every calorie."

Looking at Pat's lean frame, Devon had to smile.
He had always been tall and lanky. Now, at thirty-four
he was still perfectly proportioned while so many
friends were starting to sag around their beltlines.
From where she sat she couldn't see an ounce of

unwanted flesh. She shook herself. Where did that thought come from?

The dog stretched from where she had been laying at Devon's feet. She nuzzled Devon, expecting some treat. "Poor Dorky. Doesn't Daddy ever feed you?" Devon asked, teasing Pat. He grimaced, having already watched the dog beg two hot dogs and a burger.

"Dorky?" Sunny asked. "I thought her name was Pandora."

"It is," Pat told her, giving Devon an accusing look.

Devon laughed. "Pat named her Pandora for her curiosity. After the Dorkster destroyed his garage and ate every pair of shoes he owned, Dorky seemed more appropriate."

Sunny shook her head. "How could you name such a pretty baby Dorky?" she cooed and held out her hand. Dorky politely sniffed her fingers and whined before returning to Devon's side and laying her head on Devon's lap.

Dan told Sunny, "If you'd bribed her with food for years, she'd be loyal to you, too."

"The same could be said of some men," Devon told him.

Sunny held out a piece of meat to the dog. Dorky whined and sniffed the food, then looked to Devon in confusion. She obviously sensed the tension between the two women. The dog finally accepted the meat with the tip of her tongue, barely touching Sunny's fingers, then trotted down to the river's edge to bury it. Devon began clearing plates and Pat rose to help her. Sunny stayed firmly in her seat as the obvious clean-up effort continued. Devon shrugged. It was better than having her underfoot. Devon dried the dishes while Pat washed, then she removed the rich, buttery, chocolate bars she brought for dessert from the refrigerator. Testing the creamy frosting, she swatted Pat's hand away before he could snitch one. "Speaking of chowhounds," she teased as she headed out the door.

The four of them sat in silence as the last rays of the sun faded from the sky. The river bubbled along, even as the deepening shadows made the sound seem eerie as though it came from some unseen force just beyond their reach. Birds called in twilight songs while a gentle breeze rustled the trees, causing Devon to reach for her favorite sweatshirt. Pulling on the battered Gonzaga University shirt was more a defense against the mosquitoes now, but it wouldn't be long before the mountain air took on a deeper chill.

"Did you go to Gonzaga?" Sunny asked in surprise. The Spokane university was known as Lawyer U. in the Northwest.

"No. I went to the University of Arizona. Pat gave me this when he was in college."

Pat smiled with her at the memory. She had started her freshman year in high school as an awkward, gangly redhead and Pat had given her his sweatshirt. He hadn't said it but they had both known she would taunt her schoolmates that *she* had a boyfriend in college. Only her closest friends had known he was more like a big brother. Dan lit a table lantern and plunked down a battered game of Clue.

Pat groaned. "I hate this game."

"You just hate losing to me," Devon taunted. "You'd think after this many years, you'd be used to it."

"In your dreams," Pat returned.

Devon stuck her tongue out and reached for Miss Scarlet just as Sunny grabbed it. Devon resisted the urge to snatch it back and graciously took Mrs. White instead, thinking if the woman won with her lucky marker, she was fish bait tomorrow.

Pat took Professor Plum as he had for years and Dan took Colonel Mustard. Each player marked their pads with the concentration of NATO representatives at a world peace summit. On Sunny's turn, she moved into the ballroom. Placing the purple peg beside the red one, she smiled at Pat. "Care to dance? We *are* in the ballroom."

Pat chuckled. "It sounds like a deadly invitation to me."

Devon shot a worried glance at Dan. "Don't forget to choose your weapon," she reminded Sunny.

"How could I forget," Sunny muttered as she placed the rope alarmingly near the white marker. Dan made a sound suspiciously like a chuckle. Devon kicked him under the table for good measure.

"Ow!" he yelped, rubbing his shin. "I mean . . . wow! Look at the size of those mosquitoes." He shot Devon a furious look.

Sunny responded by slapping vigorously at her arms.

"They're the size of B-52s. What do you guys feed them?"

"Blonds," Devon told her cheerfully.

Pat cleared his throat and sent Devon a warning look. "Maybe you should put on something with long sleeves?"

"It's a good idea not to give them too much of a target," Devon chimed in helpfully.

Sunny muttered something under her breath as she rose.

"What was that?" Devon asked sweetly.

"I said, 'Go to the hall,'" she pointed at the board and returned Devon's angelic smile. "I'm sure you'll find a murder weapon there."

After she left, an uncomfortable silence fell over the porch. Pat finally cleared his throat. "I know we're trying to discourage her, but could we get through the weekend without killing each other?" he asked.

Devon felt a painful flush creep over her cheeks. She was behaving badly and she knew it. This whole weekend was a mistake and she deeply regretted agreeing to the charade. When was she going to learn to ignore Dan's great ideas? Devon sighed. "I'm sorry. I guess it has been a long week."

Pat reached over and squeezed her hand, his long fingers wrapping around her slender ones. "This weekend probably wasn't a good idea," he said thoughtfully.

"Of course not. It was Devon's idea," Dan said.

"It was not," she shot back. "Jerk."

"Witch."

Devon stuck her tongue out.

Pat shook his head. "Sometimes I forget how mature you both have become as adults."

As Sunny walked out, her eyes glanced over their clasped fingers. Pat withdrew his hand. "Perhaps we should turn in," Pat said. "It's going to be an early morning."

Devon agreed and helped clear the board, then walked into the cabin, only to freeze as she started toward the bedroom. Feeling like an awkward teenager she looked helplessly at Dan. He grinned like a fool. "Hey Pat! Where should Devon sleep?"

Devon considered strangling the wretch but opted instead for a slow painful death tomorrow when she could hide the body. Pat pointed toward the right bedroom. "She's in with Sunny. I didn't think she'd want to put up with your snoring."

Devon knew perfectly well the couch in the living room was a sofa sleeper so there was no shortage of sleeping accommodations. For that matter, she had spent many summer nights on the porch, watching the stars and listening to the water. For some reason though, she felt absurdly relieved that she was the one sleeping with their lovely guest. What was the matter with her? With a mumbled goodnight, she walked to the bedroom and noticed the amazing cosmetic arsenal on the dresser. *If Dan thinks I'm bad, he should see this,* she thought.

She quickly brushed her teeth, then scrambled into the bottom of one set of bunk beds. Sunny came in a few minutes later and slid into the lower bunk on the opposing wall. Silence stretched in the small room into a palpitating thing. Devon rolled over and tried to go to sleep. Instead her mind was whirling around. She tried to decide what it was that irritated her about their guest. Sunny was beautiful, and she seemed intelligent enough. There was something in her eyes that made Devon wonder uncomfortably if she wasn't much more intelligent than she appeared.

In fact, there was something about her that just didn't ring true, as though she were trying too hard. Surely a woman with those looks would know better than to hunt a man. She should know as a genuine beauty that she could probably sit back and have every man in the county falling for her. Odd, if she wanted to capture the McKenzie Man, she certainly seemed to be going about it all wrong.

The McKenzie Man. Somehow the curse didn't seem so amusing now. It really was a bother to Pat, she told herself firmly. He just wasn't the type to enjoy being hounded by so many women. Not that he hadn't dated his share of beautiful women over the years, but none really seemed right for him. Now he was beginning to develop a case of paranoia that would probably make him a bachelor for the rest of his life. Unless he met a woman who couldn't take a hint. That might be Pat's one failing. He would be too nice to really hurt some-one like that. That would be awful, Devon thought. She would much rather be told someone wasn't interested than making a fool of herself over someone who didn't want her. That would be too humiliating.

Not that she couldn't understand why women were making fools of themselves over Pat. He was a great guy. A woman couldn't find a nicer man, stable and sincere. In every aspect of his life there was a sense of integrity that Devon always admired. When she dangled on the winds of fate, rushing headfirst into things, Pat was a steady force. In turn she kept him from being entirely too serious. It was that blending of opposites that made them perfect friends. Friends. That funny feeling started in the pit of her stomach again. She was really lucky to have a friend like Pat. With that thought she hit her pillow and tried to get some sleep.

An eternity later, Devon had to admit it was useless. Pressing the button to illuminate her watch, she could see it was past midnight. So much for a restful weekend in the country, she thought. The breathing from the other bunk came in a quiet rhythm now. Devon slipped from the bed and crept out of the cabin. With a deep breath of relief she stood on the porch, savoring the night air she loved so much here. Moonlight reflected in flashes of silver in the water's blackness. A night owl's call wafted through the valley, eerie and beautiful, and a shadow moved near her, nearly scaring her heart from her chest.

"Sorry." Pat's soft whisper soothed her. "I didn't mean to startle you."

"What are you doing out here? Dan's snoring too much?"

Pat chuckled. "No." He took a deep breath. "I just couldn't sleep. How about you?"

"Me neither. I always liked it out here better."

Pat held his hand to her and wordlessly she slipped her fingers into his. As they walked down to the water's edge, their footsteps sounded hollow on the wooden planking of the dock.

Devon sat at the edge and pulled her shoes off to dangle her feet into the bracing water. The cold made her breath catch for a moment, then she relaxed as the water numbed her skin. Dorky padded after them, flopping down in the middle of the dock. Clasping his hands on his drawn-up knees, Pat sat next to Devon. In silence, they watched the water dance and cajole its way downstream. The sound bubbled and played as the trees rustled softly overhead.

"Remember the water fairies?" Devon asked softly.

Pat nodded in the shadows. "They're busy tonight."

Devon splashed her foot out of the water, making little ripples that were quickly swallowed by the water. No amount of science in her pursuit of two architectural degrees could convince her there weren't river fairies, at least here in this place. Now she sat here with the oddest feeling in her stomach. She had an image of Pat sitting here someday with another little girl, one with golden curls instead of red and explaining to her where the water goes. She swallowed the lump in her throat. Things change. It was one of those lessons one was supposed to learn when she grew up. She knew that. Really, she did. But still the sense of loss was keen.

Chapter Three

"**O**kay, rise and shine, sleepyheads. The fish are waiting."

Devon groaned and pulled the covers over her head. It was still pitch dark in the room. The next thing she knew, the covers were yanked off and she was glowering at Dan's hovering shadow.

"Come on. Hurry up. Ten minutes to eat, then we hit the water," he said, unceremoniously turning the light on and shaking Sunny's shoulder. Sunny sat up looking bewildered. She looked at her watch and then gave Dan a disgusted look that Devon envied. She could have used that look a few times over the years with Dan.

"You have got to be kidding," Sunny told him.

"Nope, and if you're not up in ten minutes when we

leave, Pat will drag you out, as is. Just ask Devon," he said with an impish grin.

Devon met Sunny's look and nodded. "He's not kidding. But surely you know what a morning person dear Pat can be." Grimacing at him, Sunny pushed back the covers and sucked in her breath at the shock of cold air. Devon had never thought she would appreciate Pat's early morning energy, but at this moment, it did have its merit.

"You eat," Sunny growled. "I'm going to shower."

Devon hauled her body out of bed and stretched every muscle, trying to wake up. She brushed her hair back into a ponytail and put on a warm sweat suit. The smell of something wonderful lured her to the kitchen. Pat flipped the last pancake onto the stack while Dan finished pouring the coffee. Devon bit into a piece of bacon and muttered, "What is this, her last meal?" Dan just smiled, then raised his eyebrows in mock innocence.

"She'll be in there forever," Devon grumbled.

"Not without hot water she won't," Dan told her.

"Excuse me?" Devon demanded.

"We forgot to turn the hot water heater on last night."

Neither of the men said a word as a shriek came from the bathroom, then Devon had to give the woman credit when she heard the water running anyway. She wouldn't face the cabin's mountain spring water for any man, least of all the two looking so cheerful across from her at the table. "You will take care of that won't you?" she asked them dryly.

"It's already on," Pat promised. The water stopped

running just when they finished washing dishes and Pat went to hurry Sunny along. He appeared two minutes later with a barely dressed and still damp Sunny who looked beautiful if slightly frozen.

"What smells so good?" she asked, giving Devon a black look as she rubbed her arms and shivered.

Devon shrugged. It wasn't her fault and if Sunny chose to blame her, so much the better. It wasn't like they would ever end up best friends. In fact, the sooner this weekend ended the better. Devon could only hope she never saw the witch again.

Pat answered cheerfully, "Sorry slowpoke. You took too long. If we don't hit the lake before the sun's up, we won't catch any fish."

"Too bad," she muttered under her breath.

Sunny visibly shivered as the cold mountain air hit her on the porch. Barely enough light peaked across the sky to see where they were going as the foursome walked to the dock. Devon was grateful for her heavy sweats by the time they reached the boats. Dan stood on the ground beside his canoe. "Hey, Devi! Feel up to grabbing a paddle this early?"

Devon groaned and pulled on a life vest. "Sure. Just don't blame me if I refuse to save your drowning hide in this water."

Pat shrugged. "I guess that leaves the two of us," he told Sunny. He held out a hand for her with one foot propped in the shallow fishing boat. The little boat dipped as she stepped in and Devon clapped her hands over her eyes, waiting for the splash. None came as she looked up to see Sunny sitting safely, snapping on her own life jacket.

Dorky whined from the dock. She looked to Pat, and then to Devon. "Go with Devon," Pat told her. He shrugged at Devon's questioning look. "It will be impossible to fish with her splashing around." Pushing the aluminum boat from the dock, Pat waved good-bye and headed upstream, the little motor sputtering and protesting in the early darkness. Devon rubbed her hand over her stomach as a funny quiver went through her system again. *Must have been the bacon,* she thought, watching the two figures disappear down the darkened alley of water. The dog nuzzled Devon's hand, whining as her master faded from view.

"Let's go," Dan said softly. He gave her an odd look. "They'll be fine. Pat's a good swimmer if she decides to drown him."

"I'm not worried," she lied as she boosted the dog aboard, then helped push the canoe in. The icy water splashed the side of the canoe while she shot Dan a look doubting his sanity and possibly his lineage for making her do this. "How come we're not going upstream?" she asked.

Dan paddled for a moment. "I thought this would be fun."

"And how are we going to get home?" she asked as her brain finally began to wake up. Usually they drove the canoe upstream by car, then paddled home. The water was pretty choppy this time of year and Devon didn't think it would be much fun to try paddling upstream.

"Pat helped me drive the Jeep to a spot downstream this morning," he told her, giving the passing riverbank unusual attention.

"My, weren't we up conniving early this morning." A thought struck her. That meant that Pat had purposely gotten rid of them this morning, taking Sunny the opposite direction.

She thought of the way the sultry woman looked in the moonlight last night and swallowed the lump in her throat. Maybe Dan was right and they just needed the right atmosphere. She looked upstream at the trees hanging over the river, creating a natural tunnel of peace and beauty. They couldn't ask for a better atmosphere.

"Hey, keep paddling up there," Dan called, absurdly cheerful this morning as they moved farther from the subject of Devon's thoughts.

After two hours of playing in the water, paddling upstream where they could and following the rapids where they couldn't, they decided to take a break. Dan pulled the canoe out on a wide spot while Devon picked up the small ice chest. "What did you bring to make this worthwhile?" she asked, opening the box. "Almond croissants and a thermos of coffee. Not a bad start," she acknowledged.

The morning sun was beginning to sparkle across the river valley. Golden glints of light feathered across an old Pacific Oak near them, creating a halo for an empty robin's nest while a squirrel chattered nearby. Devon tossed a piece of croissant to the fluffy little squirrel. He scampered warily a few feet, watched the dog splashing madly in the river and darted forward again. Devon laughed as he chattered furiously, reading them the riot act before snatching the crumb and flitting off to a safe distance. The dog scampered after the squirrel, barking madly when she couldn't climb the tree after the potential playmate. Devon called Dorky back, laughing, as the dog raced toward her, then forgot what she was doing and began chasing her tail.

Two years ago a jealous girlfriend dumped Pat, claiming she couldn't compete with his friendship with Devon. Devon gave Pat a tiny, golden puppy and teasingly told him the dog might be the most faithful female in his life. He still insisted on calling her Pandora, but everyone else followed Devon's example and called her Dorky. Now, Dorky was nearly ninety pounds and every ounce was trying to go in six different directions. She finally gave up and settled next to Devon, panting and looking longingly at the last piece of croissant. Devon obliged and rubbed her ears while the dog inhaled the treat without even tasting it.

A faint tang of pine mingled with the coffee and cinnamon scents. Devon absently swirled her travel mug, her mind wandering haphazardly to the times she had sat here with a different brother, enjoying the forest's morning routine.

"Wonder how Pat's making out," Dan said, while Devon marveled at his poor choice of words.

"I'm sure he's making out just fine," she snapped.

"Isn't this what you wanted when you got him into this mess?"

"Me?" she asked in disbelief.

"Yeah. You thought he needed a wife. So what's wrong with Sunny? She's pretty and she understands his job. And she seems pleasant except where you are concerned."

"Is that my fault?" Devon growled.

"Well, you weren't exactly nice to her," he admonished.

"Me!" she glowered, wondering how Dan could so quickly change sides.

Dan watched the squirrel with marked interest. "Funny. I always thought you'd be best friends with Pat's wife, close as sisters." He shrugged. "Guess not though."

"No, I guess not," Devon echoed.

Pat was in ecstacy. His eyes sparkled with pleasure and his skin flushed with the beauty of life. The air was pure, the water cold, and life was good. He had caught a fish—a big, glorious, beautiful trout and was reeling it in. Using the delicate precision of a surgeon, he pulled and gave, pulled and gave. With a sigh of complete satisfaction, he hauled the madly flipping, gyrating trout into the boat. Sunny cried out as its slithery body showered her with river water then flapped wildly in her face.

"Whoa! Sit down," Pat shouted. She did, but just

short of capsizing them. He held the beautiful fish before her proudly while its shining eye looked her over.

Sunny leaned as far back as she could without falling out of the boat. Pat pulled himself from gleeful reverie to notice the distraught look on her face. Unhooking the fish, he put it carefully in his creel as though it were made of delicate crystal. Then he wiped his hands and reached in the cooler, handing her a soda and opening one for himself. They drank for a moment while he noticed her hands were trembling.

Finally Pat shook his head. "I take it you don't do much fishing?"

He injected enough humor in his voice that Sunny started to chuckle and then they both shared a shaky laugh. "No, I'm afraid freezing my tush off in the middle of nowhere to murder some poor creature is not my idea of a fun date," Sunny told him.

Pat could feel a pink flush creeping up his neck.

"But then, that was the idea, wasn't it?" she said.

He paused for a moment, turning the can in his hands. Finally he nodded. "I'm sorry. I'm afraid I was feeling rather . . ."

"Hunted," she offered with a wry grin.

He shot her a thoughtful look. Sunny looked relaxed, more relaxed than he had seen her since she temporarily joined his office last week. Her eyes lit with humor and a slight dimple peaked at the corner of her mouth. If she had been this easygoing at work, he wouldn't have succumbed to Dan's insane plan for the weekend. "Something like that," he admitted.

Sunny looked at the scenery and seemed to be considering. "Can you tell me something? Was this weekend your idea?"

Pat shifted uncomfortably. "No. But I agreed to it."

"Under duress?" she asked.

He nodded. "I should have known better. Dan's ideas are always a disaster."

Sunny looked surprised. "I thought it was Devon's idea."

Pat shook his head. "No, she didn't want to either."

"Doesn't she like fishing?"

Pat chuckled. "If she doesn't, she keeps it to herself. Dan would have tormented her long ago if she didn't seem to love it."

"Smart girl."

"Yes, she is," Pat said with a certain amount of pride.

"Are you in love with her?" Sunny asked suddenly. It was her turn to give him a pointed look as he jerked in the boat, causing it to tilt sharply in the water.

Good heavens, where did that come from? Then he reminded himself that Sunny hadn't grown up with the Kellys and Lawrences. She didn't have the history to know the answer to that question. And she couldn't possibly know that it was a question he had begun to ask himself lately as well. "No—yes—I mean, I love her like a sister. We've grown up together."

Sunny gave him a long look. Pat had the uncomfortable feeling she could see into his thoughts. She nodded once and then looked at the trees. "She and Dan seem to spark a lot. I take it they are more than just friends?"

"No. They just spark a lot." Pat grinned at the sudden memory. "There was that one summer, though."

"What summer?"

He shook his head.

"Come on. If I don't die of hypothermia, I promise to keep it secret."

He laughed. "It's no secret. They were quite an item one summer in college, but then . . ." He shrugged.

"What happened?"

"Nobody knows."

"Hmm. Sounds like Miss Scarlet and Mr. Green tried murder in the library," Sunny quipped.

Pat laughed in return. "Probably. Whatever happened, they both get really embarrassed when anybody mentions it."

"So everyone mentions it a lot," she guessed.

"Only those of us who love them enough," he agreed.

Sunny finished her soda and handed him the empty can to store. "Well, do you think you've murdered enough poor little fishies this morning?"

"I think so. Enough for lunch anyway." He started the boat's small, outboard engine.

"Great," she shuddered. "I may become a vegetarian."

Devon was biting her nails. She hadn't done that since junior high. She looked at her watch and grimaced. Now she knew how her mother felt when Devon had gone on a date in high school. Pat had been gone hours. Maybe he had drowned. Maybe they had gotten lost . . . On a river that goes in one direction and that Pat grew up on? Not likely.

The other possibility floated through her mind. The image of Pat and Sunny locked in a heated embrace had her biting what was left of her nails. Then she heard the boat motor and looked up from her seat on the porch in relief. She grabbed her magazine and opened it quickly. After a moment, she stole a quick look to see Pat helping Sunny from the boat. Sunny wore Pat's sweater and laughed delightedly at something he had said.

Devon buried her head in the magazine again, then quickly turned it right side up. Dan came whistling out of the cabin. "How was the fishing?"

"Fine," Sunny called. "Pat caught enough to feed an army."

"You haven't seen Dan eat," Pat teased her.

"You're right," she joked back. "There's just enough, Dan."

Devon stared at Pat and Sunny in morbid fascination. They were definitely on friendlier terms than they had been this morning. It's a good thing they brought lunch, because Devon's stomach was starting to flutter again.

She noticed Dan wasn't whistling anymore. In fact, he suddenly didn't look like he was feeling any better than she was at the moment. He gave her a distressed look while she shrugged. He had been the one to suggest Sunny might be the one. He could just jump in the river if he expected any sympathy from her.

"I guess the girls better start cleaning them," Dan said. He opened the grill and began preparing it.

Pat looked at Sunny, then grinned. "That's okay. I'll clean them."

Dan was adamant. "If you caught the fish, the girls should clean them."

Devon gave him a disgruntled look. "I don't remember you catching anything."

Dan gazed at her with exasperation and tilted his head toward Sunny. Devon sighed. That was part of the plan. Torture the woman, even if she didn't necessarily feel like taking her frustration out on some helpless fish.

"Really, it's okay. I'll clean them," Pat offered.

Devon gave him a suspicious look.

"Devi is the best fish filleter in the county," Dan told Sunny.

"I'll be sure to include that in my resumé," Devon told him.

"Well. I guess I should learn from the best," Sunny said. She took the line of fish gingerly.

"Devi can show you where we clean them," Dan said, then turned back to the grill, whistling merrily again.

Devon led her to a shed beside the cabin. A wide shelf had been built into the side of the building, perfect for the grisly task ahead. Devon picked up a knife and handed one to Sunny. Sunny looked a little green about the gills.

"It's easy. Just two quick cuts," Devon sliced the trout with the ease of years of experience. "Then a little slit here and you pull. Voila!"

Sunny made a gurgling sound in her throat.

"Here you try," Devon offered. Sunny gave her a disbelieving look and Devon wondered at the wisdom of giving her a sharp knife. Then the other woman gingerly picked up the slippery fish.

"Cutting its throat is the worst part," Devon offered helpfully.

"I would imagine so," Sunny muttered. She tried to imitate Devon's quick work but took several tries before she could even get a firm grip on the fish.

"They're dead. It's not going to hurt them," Devon told her, starting to see the wisdom in Dan's plan. Sunny looked positively revolted. "Pat did a great job. He's really quite the fisherman. He'd be up here every weekend if he could," she told Sunny.

She could hear Sunny's teeth grinding as she started to attack the fish. "Bleah!" she made a face and handed what was left of the disfigured vertebrate to Devon.

"Well," Devon said, having finished the rest of the catch. "I guess it's not bad for a first time." She dumped the cleaned fish in a newspaper and reached for a garden hose hanging nearby. She cranked the water on, thinking the water pressure from the well would be low after a couple weeks of disuse. Unfortunately, she was wrong and the water shot out, blasting the shelf and splattering Sunny with dirty fish water, among other things.

Devon stopped in horror as the young woman sputtered helplessly. Sunny's eyes narrowed as she looked at Devon. Sunny started to lunge for the hose just as Devon, for some unearthly reason, said, "Here, let me help you wash that off," and turned the hose on Sunny.

The other woman shrieked as the icy water hit her in the chest. Sunny grabbed the hose and the two of them grappled while icy water sprayed madly over them. Just as Devon lunged to turn the nozzle off, Sunny wrestled the hose from her and her feet shot out from under her. The two women went down in a tangle of arms and legs.

Devon sat up when the shock of the cold water subsided and looked at the scene of the crime. She and Sunny were covered with mud and heaven only knew what else. Sunny's perfect hair was sticking up in spikes with bits of mud splattered across her face. Her white T-shirt was now brown and there was no hope for the designer shorts she wore. Devon tried to hide the snicker, but couldn't. If she were going to be murdered, at least she'd go out laughing. Even more shocking though, Sunny looked down at herself and joined Devon's laughter. In a matter of minutes the two were laying on the ground pointing at each other, laughing hysterically. It was only the sight of a pair of man's legs that brought Devon sitting upright.

"Hello Pat," Sunny sputtered.

He arched an eyebrow at the two of them. "I take it one cold shower wasn't enough?" he asked her. Their beautiful guest snorted in return which started both women laughing again.

"Anything I can do?" That had the two of them back on the ground, clutching their sides with mirth. "Hmm. I guess not," he said before picking up the fish and walking away, still shaking his head.

When she could finally breathe again, Devon helped Sunny to her feet. "I'm sorry." She grinned at the look Sunny gave her. The animosity between the two had for the moment been replaced by something a little more friendly. "Really, I am."

Sunny tried to wipe some of the goo off and made it worse. "I'm sorry, too. I didn't know Pat was spoken for. Otherwise I would never have—"

"Pat's not," Devon interrupted before she thought. "I mean, he's not . . . umm . . ."

"It's okay. I can see the two of you have something going on," Sunny said with her head down, swiping at her shorts.

Devon shook her head madly, sending bits of water spraying about. "No. Pat and I are just friends."

"Right," Sunny said in a tone that said she obviously didn't believe it. "And I'm the world's best fish cleaner."

"No," Devon grinned. "But you might be the world's messiest."

Sunny sighed. "I suppose this means another cold shower."

Devon had to be honest. "There's probably lots of hot water by now."

"I see. And whose idea was that?"

Devon raised her hands in innocence. "It was an accident. I'm not that mean." Sunny looked down at herself and gave Devon such a look of disbelief that they both started laughing again. "Okay, maybe I am, but cold showers are definitely below the belt," Devon said.

Devon used Pat's shower while Sunny cleaned up. There really wouldn't be any hot water left by the time they finished, she thought. She had to scrub three times just to get the fish smell off. Apparently deodorant soaps were not meant to kill aroma-du-trout. Stepping out of the shower, she felt almost human again. She brushed her hair with Pat's brush, then, in curiosity, picked up the aftershave sitting on the vanity. Musk. No, that was Dan.

The other held a familiar, warm spicy smell. Pat. It smelled like good, clean soap with a little spice and a hint of floral mixed in. Perfect. *Just like Pat.* Devon sighed. Dan and his brilliant ideas.

Chapter Four

"Want to hunt berries?" Devon asked that afternoon. She held out a bucket to Sunny.

Sunny shook her head. "No thanks. I've trapped enough food today."

"How about a canoe trip?" Dan offered. "We could catch a ride upstream with Pat and Devon, then paddle home."

Sunny nodded. "That sounds like fun."

Dan whistled for the dog. "Want to go in the canoe?" he asked. Dorky barked and turned a complete circle in the air.

"Guess that means yes," he said. He smiled at Sunny. "You'll have to ask Devon how she keeps her calm, though. Unless you want to go swimming."

Sunny laughed. "I think I've had enough showers today. How about it, Devon? What's your secret?"

47

Devon marveled at the change in Sunny. She seemed more relaxed and certainly more pleasant to be around. Devon walked to the cupboard and retrieved some oatmeal cookies. The dog whined when she handed them to Sunny. Sunny offered one to Dorky then had to step over her eager new friend while the guys loaded the canoe onto Pat's SUV. When Dan slid into the back with Sunny, Devon shot Pat a cautious glance, wondering how he might react, but he grinned back at her. In no time, they left Dan and Sunny paddling downstream with a remarkably well-behaved dog, then drove further, looking for huckleberries.

"There always used to be a big patch along those power lines up the road. Why don't we start there?" Devon suggested.

"Fine. I'm glad you remembered to bring some buckets for the berries," Pat told her as they drove down the highway looking for the elusive huckleberry patch.

"Humph. Tell that to your brother. He thought it was a stupid idea to bring them."

"I guess that means he doesn't get any of the booty?"

"Darned right. That will teach him to make fun of my packing skills," she told him with very little conviction. They both knew Dan could charm every last berry from her.

"Oh, that was the turn-off," Devon said, as she realized they had just passed the power lines. Pat turned around at the next wide spot in the road and pulled onto the utility road. "I hope we're not too late. It seems like everybody in the world comes up here now to pick berries and there aren't as many patches anymore," Devon worried aloud.

"Not like us, you mean. We have a right to be here," Pat teased.

"Well, we've been doing this forever. It's not like we're newcomers," she told him.

Just as Pat picked up his bucket, Devon shouted, "Oh no! Do you believe this?"

Pat raced to her side, then grimaced when she pointed to the source of her dismay, the remains of a weekend party littered about the ground.

"I'll get the trash bag from the car," he offered.

Devon watched him trot off. He looked so comfortable here. Wearing khaki shorts and a T-shirt made him look less austere than the business clothes he wore in the city. She cocked her head as he bent into the car. *Nice tush.*

Devon snapped her attention back to the crushed beer cans and broken bits of glass, being careful not to get cut. Joining her, Pat bent to help, then immediately dropped a jagged piece of glass and held his bleeding hand.

"Oh, Pat! That looks bad," Devon told him.

"It's okay. It's just a cut."

"Have you had a tetanus shot lately?"

He gave her a blank look. "Not in years."

"We'd better get you to a hospital."

"I don't think we need to race to an emergency room," he argued. "It's hardly bleeding anymore."

Blood flowed from the cut, dripping off his hand onto one of the beer cans. Taking the white bandanna she used for her ponytail, Devon quickly wrapped the gash. She ran to the SUV and reached under the seat. She knew Pat had a first-aid kit there. She had bought it for him after the last time they went hiking and she had scraped her leg. She opened the kit and bit her lip. She had a sinking feeling Pat was better at this than she was.

Pat joined her as she pulled out the instruction book, scissors, and bug bite stick. He picked up the stick and chuckled. "I don't think we need this, honey." He handed her a gauze pad to unwrap and the small tape dispenser. She tore open an alcohol pad and started cleaning around the wound. It looked serious. Worse than the time she sliced her hand trying to cut a metal dowel rod for a shelf at home and that had needed five stitches. "I think the hospital in Bend is probably faster. If we leave now we can be there before this starts to swell."

"Can we at least pick some berries first?" he argued. "It's not like I'm going to get lockjaw in five minutes, you know."

Devon felt tears threatening at the sight of Pat's blood. She realized it was far worse to deal with some-one else's injury rather than your own. She gave him a wobbly smile. "I don't know. If you start howling at the moon, I'm out of here."

"Thank you so much. I'll remember that on our next trip to urgent care for you," he told her.

She stuck her tongue out at him, then tried again. "Pat, please, could we go to the hospital? You know I hate the sight of blood."

He grinned and feigned surprise. "Really? I'd think you'd be used to it. You and Dan have drawn enough blood over the years." She gave him her best pleading look and he finally sighed and gave in. "Let's get enough berries for dinner, then—I promise—we'll go to a hospital."

In gratitude, she reached up to kiss him on the cheek just as he turned his head to pick up the bucket. Her lips landed on his while their eyes widened in shock. They stood looking at each other, then Pat placed his good hand on her cheek. Devon closed her eyes as he leaned forward. Whatever she was expecting to feel, it wasn't this as his lips softly touched hers.

No wonder women chase him, she thought dreamily. *He tastes like moonlight.* An image of the women who had thrown themselves at him careened through her brain like a blast of cold water. Raising shaking fingers to her lips, she stepped back, trying to catch her breath. She was absolutely, positively not going to become some silly female chasing her best friend just because of a curse!

She started to apologize to Pat but he had the strangest look on his face, like he had never seen her before. She didn't blame him. Maybe she could blame it on some alien possession or something, because she would certainly never consider kissing Pat the way she had just kissed him. What on earth had she been thinking?

"Sorry," she told him, trying to steady her voice. "I'll start over here." She picked up her bucket and bolted for the nearest huckleberry bush. After twenty minutes of strained silence, Devon noticed Pat grimacing when he shifted the bucket of berries.

"I'm done. I think I have enough berries for dessert tonight and breakfast. Why don't we go to Bend now?"

"Why don't we go back to the cabin and put these berries in the fridge? I'll wash this cut and if we need to, then I'll go the hospital," he told her.

"Patrick Michael Lawrence, you promised," she told him testily.

He sighed. "I did, but it doesn't even hurt anymore. It's probably fine."

Devon unwrapped the bandage and peeked at the cut. It had stopped bleeding, but, if anything, it looked worse.

"Oh, Pat. You have to go to the hospital. That looks awful."

"Some nurse you would make. You're supposed to tell me it doesn't look bad and give me a bullet to bite," he teased her.

Devon reached in his pocket to get his car keys before he could waste any more time arguing. He flinched and cleared his throat. "What are you doing?"

"Driving you to the hospital."

Pat gave her an amused look. "Wouldn't it be faster if I drove? I won't get lost."

"You're hurt," she argued, wondering why she bothered with an attorney.

"It's not that big of a deal." He reached for the keys, then grimaced as he flexed his hand. "You promise you won't get lost?" Pat asked doubtfully.

Dan was usually the one who teased her, saying she couldn't find her way out of a paper bag. Unfortunately, it was true. She knew she had the most dismal sense of direction on earth. "No problem," she told him. "Besides, you can be in charge of navigating."

Devon slid into the driver's seat and immediately found herself looking up at the car ceiling. The seat back was tipped so far down, the only thing keeping her from sliding to the floor was the steering wheel jammed six inches below the seat. She clawed her way up using the steering wheel for leverage, only to peer like a child over the dashboard. Devon had always prided herself on her long legs, but even wiggling her toes, she couldn't reach the gas pedal. Trying to stay upright, she decided Pat had the seat bottom tilted all the way up so he wouldn't slide under the dashboard when he got in. The steering wheel was so low, it wedged her knees into a Chinese torture position.

It was obvious that Pat was a sadist and Devon had never realized it before. It took several minutes to fight and threaten the seats into a humane position. Pat sat patiently looking at her while his right eyebrow nearly disappeared into his hairline. "Problems?" he asked.

"How can you possibly drive like this?" Devon asked in exasperation as she finally adjusted the mirror and started the car.

"There's nothing wrong with the way I drive and now it's going to take half an hour to get my seat comfortable again," he told her.

"Excuse me. I must have failed Human Pretzels 101 in college, but I'm sure that after ten minutes in this car I would need a good chiropractor."

She looked at Pat out of the corner of her eye and saw that he had that goofy grin he had always given her. When she was younger it meant he was about to ruffle her hair. Now she just felt a lump climbing to her throat. She mentally shook herself and prayed she wouldn't get lost. Miraculously, they not only found Bend, but the hospital. Devon silently thanked the city planners for their wealth of information signs. The receptionist on duty smiled as she looked up at Devon, then smiled even more when she noticed the handsome man next to her. Pat smiled back politely.

"Is there a doctor available?" Devon asked. She might as well have asked the wall. The woman was gazing rather rapturously into Pat's green eyes. Devon risked a glance herself. At the moment they were a little cloudy from pain, but they really were beautiful. She shook herself.

"Excuse me," Devon tried again. "He's been injured." This got the nurse's attention. "He's bleeding a lot." She was getting into this now. If she said he was about to drop dead, they might even see a doctor today.

"Of course. We just need to get some information in our computer." She handed Devon a stack of papers on a clipboard. "We'll need signatures and insurance information on these." Devon reached into Pat's back pocket and pulled out his wallet. She flipped it open to his insurance card and handed it to the woman, then started filling out the forms for him. She quickly answered the questions. No allergies, one hospitalization for appendicitis, no current medications. It suddenly struck her how intimate a thing it was to fill out someone's health information. It was probably even more odd how easy it was for her. You learn a lot about someone when you've known him forever, she realized.

"Was your last tetanus shot on that camping trip after college?" she asked him. She glanced up when he didn't answer right away. "Pat? Are you okay?"

He nodded, then swallowed hard. "Yes. That was, what, twelve years ago?"

She nodded as an odd look came over his face again, like he had never seen her. She squeezed his hand in reassurance. He really wasn't handling this well, she thought. Devon finished the form and handed it back. The receptionist was glancing between the two of them. "It will just be a minute if you and your wife would like to wait."

"Oh, we're not married. I mean, we're just friends," Devon stammered. The woman looked at his wallet, held so easily in her hand and then to Pat. Devon sighed as she turned away from the receptionist's desk. How many times had people mistaken their friendship for something more over the years?

The emergency room doors opened and a young couple walked in. The man had his arms protectively around her enormous middle as she waddled uncomfortably forward. The receptionist rushed forward with a wheelchair. "Back so soon?" she asked.

The young man nodded, his face drained of color. "By the time we got home, the contractions were three minutes apart. We came right back."

"That's a good sign. She'll be fine," she assured him. A nurse hurried forward and welcomed the two, trying to put the young man at ease, as he looked like he might need the wheelchair at any moment.

Devon smiled as the couple was hustled down the hall. "He looked worse than his wife," she whispered to Pat. Again, he gave her that funny look. In fact, he didn't look a whole lot better than the soon-to-be father.

"Pat, are you all right?"

He nodded. "I guess I'm used to being here for you," he said.

"Yes, well, there was that summer you practically memorized my insurance information," she teased him. She bit her lip as his eyes seemed to take in every detail of her face. He was acting so strangely. She hoped the doctor saw him soon. He was starting to worry her.

A nurse called his name and motioned for them to follow. She led them to a small examining room. "You look very familiar," she told him.

Pat shook his head. "I live in Eugene. We were just out picking huckleberries when I got cut."

A look of recognition suddenly came over her face. "You're the McKenzie Man!" she exclaimed in a delighted voice. "Our newspaper did an article about the curse last week. And now I get to meet the guy who's going to break the McKenzie Man curse." Devon flushed as she realized the dubious distinction Pat had gained. The nurse checked Pat's blood pressure and took his temperature while flirting outrageously with him. She was old enough to be his mother, but Devon wondered if there was some chemical reaction that happened when a man was captured by the curse. Not that things were any different before then. Pat's easy temperament and striking good looks had always attracted women of all shapes and sizes. He was just a genuinely nice guy and that hadn't changed through the mayhem this year. Devon sighed, hoping maybe his celebrity status might get him some real medical attention before he was old enough to be a grandfather.

Within minutes, the doctor walked in, pulling the drapes closed behind him. He was young, but seemed nice enough. He gave Devon an encouraging smile as she stood next to Pat. That was more like it. At least this medical professional wouldn't be sewing Pat's arm to his ear because he wasn't paying attention.

"I'm Dr. Martin," he told Devon. "Let's see what we have here," he said, carefully pulling the bandage off.

Devon bit her lip at the angry-looking cut. It had started to swell and must hurt badly. She gripped Pat's other hand tightly as the doctor examined the wound. Pat gave her fingers a reassuring squeeze. Pulling out a tray of torturous-looking devices, Dr. Martin asked Devon, "How did this happen?"

"We were looking for huckleberries," she tried to explain, looking at a particularly vicious little knife on the tray and wondering if the hospital really was a good idea.

Dr. Martin looked at the cut in amazement. "A huckleberry bush did this?"

"No," she said, gulping. The needle he was filling with some liquid loomed before her and Devon wondered if she could think of a decent excuse to leave before she fainted. Pat's fingers flexed on hers as the doctor prodded the cut. "Pat was trying to pick up some litter and a broken bottle cut him."

"Tsk, tsk." The doctor shook his head while he plunged the needle into Pat's hand. "A nasty bottle just jumped up and attacked him?"

Devon giggled, one step from hysteria. "Something like that. Is that the tetanus shot?"

"Oh no. We save the best torture for last," Dr. Martin told her, smiling charmingly while he placed Pat's hand on a table to begin work. "This will numb the area before we begin to stitch the cut. He'll probably need about eight stitches and then he'll be as good as new." Dr. Martin began to squirt liquid into the cut, cleaning it while blood poured onto the tray underneath.

Devon felt horribly warm and glanced at Pat, trying to give him a reassuring smile. For some reason he looked thunderous. Maybe he thought eight was too many stitches. He was too intelligent to blame the doctor for having to clean the cut but Devon was becoming alarmed by the ticking pulse in Pat's neck that matched the black expression on his face. She turned back to the delightful doctor, since *he* didn't look ready to kill someone. Pat certainly wasn't being a good sport about this. And it wasn't her fault the stupid bottle attacked him. And hurt him. Devon bit her lip and tried to hide the tears that filled her eyes.

"It's okay," the doctor said, reassuring Devon as he patted her arm. "He'll live."

The doctor might not, Pat thought, *if he touches her again.* If his hand wasn't in the middle of the fourth stitch and busy at the moment, he would rearrange this guy's bedside manner.

What was wrong with him? First, he had nearly stopped breathing watching her fill out his insurance forms. It was such a cozy thing that he had felt overwhelmed with the intimacy of it. Just when his heart settled down and his stomach stopped doing flip-flops, this doctor came in and started flirting with her. Now he wanted to punch a complete stranger for no earthly reason.

It wasn't like he hadn't seen her flirt with other men before. He had always watched each one, wondering if this would be the one to capture her heart, but none of them had ever been worth a second look. Why would he care if she fell in love with this guy, married him, and lived happily ever after? It was none of his business—unless the good doctor didn't appreciate her, because then the doctor would have the whole Lawrence family to answer to.

That must be it. As they had gotten older, he no longer worried about playground bullies and boys with less-than-honorable intentions. He was simply worried that Devon might not find someone who deserved her. She deserved someone who made her eyes light up with laughter. Someone who appreciated every goofy part of her. Someone that she could love forever. For some reason now his hand didn't hurt anymore, but his heart certainly did.

As Devon signed the follow-up care forms, the doctor finished bandaging the wound and gave Pat his tetanus shot. She checked the last box as the doctor taped the bandage around Pat's hand. Before Devon could even thank him properly, Pat was whisking her out of the hospital and to the parking lot. She gave him an amused look. He must truly hate being the patient from the way he practically dragged her from the nice Dr. Martin.

"You were really brave," Devon told Pat, turning the alarm off on his SUV.

He stopped her for a moment. Reaching down, he pushed a button on the side of the car seat. "There. The next time you drive, you just push button number two and it will move the seat to the position you like."

"What about the way you like it?"

"It has two controls." He grinned at her. "It makes life easier for married couples." Then he sobered and looked away.

Devon saw the lost look on his face and instinctively reached up to brush a lock of dark hair from his forehead. He really had been through a tough weekend and yet he was thinking of a little thing like a car seat control to make her happy. It was like that with Pat. Swallowing hard at the sudden tears that threatened, she couldn't do anything else but hug him. "I'm sorry you got hurt," she said, repeating words of comfort he had offered her in a hospital twenty years earlier while a doctor looked at her broken arm.

Pat hugged her back. "I'm fine, Devi. It doesn't even hurt."

She could feel his cheek on the top of her head and hear his heart beating. He was hurt, but still offering her comfort. She looked up at him, her best friend in the world. "I really didn't know huckleberries could be so deadly."

Pat chuckled. "Only you could turn berry picking into an adventure." He kissed the top of her head gently. "Thank you," he whispered.

"For what?"

"For making me laugh."

She looked at his eyes crinkled with humor and tender care, the look she had seen so many times before. This was what mattered. This fierce friendship and love they shared. Preserving it was something she had taken for granted, but never again. Nothing should come between their friendship.

"You're welcome," she told him softly. Something

flared in his eyes, something that made her stomach flutter. Devon pulled away. "Do you want to get a cup of coffee?" she asked briskly.

He looked at his watch. "We should probably head back." He grinned at Devon. "If not, Dan will start cooking dinner."

Devon reached for the car keys. "Good point. We can't exactly order pizza at the cabin."

"Do you want me to drive?" he asked.

"Hey, I didn't even get lost," she protested.

"True. I don't feel like pushing our luck though," he told her, grinning as he settled into the passenger seat.

"Sit back and I'll take you wherever you want to go," she teased.

"Promises, promises," he said softly, an odd expression crossing his face.

Devon gave him a startled look but Pat looked out the window. They drove in silence back to the cabin. Dan had started the grill, but fortunately hadn't actually tried to cook anything yet. Sunny promised to help Dan with the grill while Pat stayed in the kitchen with Devon. With one hand bandaged, he wasn't much help and stepping around him every five seconds in the small kitchen was making Devon's head pound. She threw some fruit and vegetables together and fled to the patio.

Dinner was infinitely more relaxed than the previous night's. Sunny sparkled with enthusiasm as she described their day canoeing. Gone was the sultry, clinging blond Pat had arrived with. Instead, she and Devon actually teased Pat over his traumatic huckleberry adventure. The long day wound down to a peaceful evening as the four sat watching the last rays of light fade from the river valley.

"Man, I am really tired." Dan stretched and yawned. "Time to turn in."

"Me, too," Sunny said. "I hope we aren't getting up at the crack of dawn again."

Pat shook his head. "Sleep in. You deserve it."

Devon wondered what that meant as Sunny waved goodnight and followed Dan inside. Pat dimmed the lantern and they sat in the night air, the moon and light from the cabin softly gracing the shadows.

"How's your hand?" Devon asked.

"Good. Doesn't hurt at all."

Devon chewed on her lip. Pat would say that if he had a limb amputated. He was a rare man, one who didn't whine over every little pain or setback. She wished there was something she could do to make him feel better. "Is there anything I can get you?"

"No," he said. "It'll be better in the morning."

"I hope so. You better get some rest though."

They stood up at the same time and bumped into each other. Pat's arms instinctively came around her to steady her. Devon found herself looking up into a face she had known all her life, but that had somehow changed in the past twenty-four hours. The light from inside the cabin highlighted the lean angles of his jaw and turned his normally green eyes into pools of shadow. She could have been standing next to a stranger if it wasn't for all the emotions whirling around her.

Pat reached a hand to her cheek, rubbing softly; he seemed to be noticing every feature for the first time. Slowly, ever so softly, he ran his thumb over her cheek, tracing the outline of her face. The most comfortable arms in the world surrounded her. She laid her cheek against his chest and heard the steady beat of his heart. Her hands kneaded the firm planes of his back, strong and perfectly muscled. The feeling in the pit of her stomach that had plagued her for two days burst into fullness as a fierce wanting clogged her brain. Then, Pat pulled away, gently kissing her eyes, nose, and ears before taking a shaky step back.

They drew apart and stood looking at each other, as though they'd never seen each other before. *How could this be?* This wasn't some mysterious stranger who made her pulse pound. This was Pat, the man who still rumpled her hair occasionally.

Pat started to speak, but Devon shook her head. "It's late. I'm really tired." Devon darted into the cabin before he could stop her.

In the bathroom she stood, breathing hard, as though she had run a marathon. She leaned her forehead against the mirror and closed her eyes. What just happened, did not happen. It couldn't have. She felt like she was on a sinking ship and the last lifeboat just left. The loving and special relationship she shared with Pat was in danger and she desperately wanted it back just the way it was. She looked at the woman in the mirror for reassurance and found none.

Devon woke the next morning with a groan. She felt like she hadn't gotten any sleep at all. Then she remembered why. The embrace. The memory of her heated response to him made her blush with mortification. Poor Pat. He came up here to discourage one woman and now he was probably terrified his best friend was going to pounce on him at any moment. Well, she would just have to make sure that didn't happen. They would return home and things would get back to normal. Hopefully he would forget the whole thing.

But *how do you forget a feeling like that?* Devon shook her head. Easy. She would remind herself on a daily basis that Pat was her closest friend and she absolutely was not going to drive him away. And then she was going to go on a date with someone— anyone—because obviously she had been neglecting that part of her life for too long.

This was turning out to be some weekend. Instead of feeling rested, she felt like she needed another day to recuperate. Glancing at the other bunk, she could see Sunny was already up, and judging from the steam in the bathroom, her shower must have been much more comfortable this morning. Devon showered, then took a long time getting dressed. She was going back to the city, so she bothered to put on makeup. She started to dress, wondering what would be flattering, then shook her head furiously and pulled on a clean sweatshirt.

For the first time in her life, she looked forward to leaving the cabin. A dull, throbbing ache was starting behind her eyes and her stomach jumped at the thought of eating a civilized breakfast with the other occupants of the cabin. Not all of them, just one. Sighing heavily, she opened the door. It must be a full moon, and probably some unknown comet was sailing by overhead for good measure. This weekend had just been too bizarre. Pinning a smile on her face, she emerged, ready for the whatever new disaster might be awaiting her. Things looked normal enough this morning, though. Pat was making pancakes while Sunny set the table and Dan carried bags to the car.

"Hey, sleepyhead," Dan teased. "We were wondering if you were ever going to get up."

"I had trouble getting to sleep," she admitted, then wanted to kick herself when three pairs of eyes turned to her with varying expressions of curiosity. She didn't meet any of them as she grabbed a coffee cup.

"Could you turn the ham, please?" Pat asked, holding up his bandaged hand while the other flipped a pancake.

Devon mumbled something appropriate and gingerly moved next to him in the small kitchen. Sunny came bustling in, looking for more cooking utensils. After Pat showed her the drawer, Devon had to practically move into his arms for Sunny to retrieve the forks. Sunny chatted with Pat about some case from work as Devon waited patiently for her to leave, silently counting to one hundred. She tried not to think of her bottom resting so comfortably against his hip and how she fit just perfectly under his shoulder.

If the blond would just move out of the kitchen, she wouldn't have to stand on top of Pat, she thought crossly. With a cheerful smile, Sunny stayed right where she was. To top it off, Dan had renewed his annoying habit of whistling. If she survived breakfast without scalding herself, it would be a miracle. Finally, mercifully, the ham was done and she nearly threw it onto the plate in her haste to leave the cramped quarters. Breakfast was an odd affair, with Dan and Sunny continuing in their unreasonably good moods while Pat and Devon kept their heads down, eating and answering in monosyllables. Devon left the dishes in the sink for Dan and bolted for her room to pack. Sunny joined her.

"Your adventure yesterday was certainly delicious," Sunny announced from across the room.

Devon zipped her shirt into the bag, then sat wrestling it away. "What do you mean?"

"The huckleberries. They're wonderful on pancakes."

"Ah."

"And Pat was certainly brave about his injury. Most men would cry and want you to kiss it and make it better," Sunny chatted.

Devon turned to give her a suspicious look. Sunny ducked her head, but she could see the blond's shoulders shaking. "All right. Spit it out," Devon ordered.

"Why, whatever do you mean?" Sunny mimicked the sultry voice she had used when they first met.

Devon laughed. "I mean, whatever it is you're trying not to say. Nothing happened." She could feel the blush starting at her neck and creeping to her hairline. One of the hazards of being an honest redhead.

Sunny's eyes widened. "Honestly!" Devon said quickly, then glowered when Sunny burst out laughing. Devon threw a pillow at her.

"You deserved that," Sunny told her, throwing the pillow back.

"Yes, I guess I did." Devon finished her packing and decided to tackle the question that had been bothering her for two days. "Can I ask you something?"

"You can ask," Sunny said pointedly.

"You're beautiful," Devon said honestly, "but you acted like you were desperate for Pat when you got here."

Sunny sighed and closed the door. "Is this just between us?"

Devon nodded.

"I wasn't really," Sunny continued. "I mean he's a great guy, really great, but actually—I lost a bet."

Devon's confusion must have shown.

"I lost a bet with someone on how long it would take the last McKenzie Man to get married." She shook her head in disgust. "Man, did he fall fast."

Devon murmured in agreement. "He didn't even know what hit him."

"Anyway. I had to get a date with the next one, and, of course . . ."

"It was Pat," Devon finished for her.

"Yep. He is a great guy, too great, and I was hoping if I drove him crazy we'd both be safe from *it*. You know."

"The curse."

"The one and only." Sunny shuddered.

"Ah. I take it you're not ready to settle down?" Devon asked.

Sunny shook her head adamantly, the blond waves swinging. "No. Been there too young and done that. I can live without wedding bells for awhile."

Devon sighed. "Have we apologized for how obnoxious we were?"

"Well. Dan apologized yesterday," Sunny chuckled. "But he did say most of the blame lay on your shoulders."

"I'll kill him," Devon muttered.

"He said you threaten that a lot."

"Only when he deserves it," Devon told her.

"Actually, I was more afraid Pat would file a harassment suit if this kept up. I swear I will never bet Mitch on anything again."

"The bet was with Mitch?" Devon asked in surprise.

"Yep. It would serve him right if he is the next McKenzie Man."

"Wow, you don't hold a grudge or anything do you?" Devon asked, laughing as she picked up her bag.

"I guess you'll find out," Sunny told her in an evil voice.

They both were laughing as they carried their bags outside. Pat looked at Devon for a moment as he stood at his car. Again Devon felt a sense of awkwardness as she shifted her bags. Sunny put her bags at Pat's vehicle while Dan took Devon's. He pulled her aside and asked quietly, "Want me to drive Sunny home? You could ride with Pat."

"No!" she whispered back fervently.

For some reason Dan looked absurdly pleased. If he started whistling again, Devon vowed *he* would need to see Dr. Martin.

Chapter Five

"Hello, are you still there?"

Devon's mind snapped back to Leslie's face. "Excuse me?"

Leslie Francis gave her an amused look as Devon glanced at her notepad for a clue as to their discussion and saw it was blank. Leslie was the landscape architect for the historical society, so that narrowed the choices. Hostas? Hydrangeas? Heliotropes?

"I said, how was the fishing trip?"

Devon nearly snapped the tip of her pen off. Unfortunately Leslie was also her closest girlfriend.

"So did Pat unload the femme fatale?" Leslie asked.

"Actually, she wasn't so bad," Devon said quietly, madly looking through her day planner for another topic.

71

"So she might be the one?" Leslie asked.

"No!" Devon said a bit too forcefully. "No, just nicer than I would have been under the circumstances."

"Like you'd ever be in that situation." Leslie snorted in disgust. "I can't imagine you chasing a man into paranoia, especially Pat Lawrence."

Devon swallowed hard. "No, especially not Pat."

Leslie chewed thoughtfully on the end of her drafting pencil. "It better happen pretty soon though."

"What?"

"The curse. Pat's lasted so long, it's kind of embarrassing," Leslie said, doodling orchids on her notepad. "Not that I ever thought I'd feel sorry for your big brother."

"He's not my big brother," Devon snapped in exasperation. "About the grounds?"

"Oh, sorry." Leslie pulled some landscape designs from a folder. "I've made some preliminary sketches based on what we know of the Rosemary estate. The rest can be filled in using other examples from the period. The Bush house in Salem has offered shoots from their pioneer rose garden so we'll have the real thing. With luck they'll be blooming by next summer."

She pulled out another design and Devon tried to concentrate, taking haphazard notes on her pad.

"Fort Vancouver has offered some hollyhock and housewort seeds and their horticulturist has offered to drive down and look the grounds over." Leslie stopped to peer at Devon's notes. She cleared her throat. "It's housewort, not house warts. Of course, if the house has warts, you would know. Funny, I don't remember seeing that in your architectural report."

Devon blushed and scribbled the correction.

Leslie watched her for a moment. "You don't think it affects women, do you?" she finally asked.

"I think anyone can get them. Dandelion juice is supposed to help though," Devon said absently.

"Excuse me?" Leslie asked.

"I read in one of the historical guides that dandelion juice is good for warts."

Leslie gave her the oddest look and made a strange, clearing sound in her throat. The dimple at the side of her mouth twitched. "I meant the curse. You know, the McKenzie Man. It only affects men, right?"

Devon looked at her suspiciously as Leslie tried to hide the laughter in her eyes.

"That's not funny."

"No, of course not," Leslie was grinning broadly now.

Devon dropped her head to her hands. "That's really not funny."

"Why not? He's a great guy. No surprises lurking in the closet. Probably no house warts either," Leslie teased.

Devon thought of the embrace on the porch. Any more surprises like that and she'd be in intensive care, or a mental hospital.

"I've always thought you two would be great together," Leslie told her.

Devon considered this in light of its source. Leslie was the most practical, least romantic woman she knew. In fact, in the four years they had known each other she couldn't remember Leslie ever having a serious relationship with a man. It sounded like a smart plan at this point.

But Leslie thought she and Pat were a great idea. Well, no one was perfect.

"Umm, about the warts," Devon said.

"You mean the housewort?" Leslie couldn't keep a straight face to save her soul.

It was going to be a very long day.

Chapter Six

She was late, as usual. Half their friends were probably already in the pool at Pat's house. Glancing again at the clock and wishing she could slow it, Devon finished putting pieces of fruit in the bowl, placed the brownies on a plate, grabbed her bag, and left for Pat's house, At least it wouldn't take long to get there, being just a couple blocks away. This wasn't the first time Devon appreciated Pat's proximity. Of course, it really wasn't a coincidence that he lived so close. Every day on her way to work, she had driven by the beautiful but decrepit old home and then one day, about three years ago, a "For Sale" sign appeared.

She'd needed to twist his arm just a little to convince Pat that the dirty, disreputable building could be beautiful, but in the end she won. He bought the house for a song and then stepped back while Devon went to work. Built one hundred years earlier by land-wealthy farmers, Devon teased Pat that now it was a suitable haven for an overstressed, under-worked attorney. As a smart lawyer, he knew enough not to reply. Every time she drove up to the majestic white house with *her* window boxes she felt a rush of pride. She had put a lot of herself into it, from renovating the delicately carved lattice work at the eaves to the rich, golden hardwood floors inside.

Carefully balancing her load, she pushed open the front door before Pat's overzealous golden retriever bowled her over. "Whoa! Down girl. Pat, would you call off your monster? Down, Dorky!"

"I hate that name," he muttered, capturing the dog's collar. Devon laid her dishes on the counter and turned to accept the exuberant canine kisses she knew were coming. "Too bad you're just a dog. You could teach the men in my life a thing or two about greetings," she told Dorky, ruffling her fur.

Pat chuckled. "So that's what you want? Someone to lead around on a leash. I knew it all along," he teased as he snitched one of the brownies.

Pat watched Devon greet the delirious dog, thinking there were probably plenty of men who would gladly change places with the dog. The skinny girl he knew as a kid had long since grown to a strikingly beautiful woman. Today she looked like a bright summer blossom. Taking advantage of the late summer heat wave, she was wearing shorts and a swimsuit top that showed an alarming amount of Devon. Auburn waves of hair that shone with health fell over her shoulder while she scratched the dog's side. Pandora immediately rolled onto her back, knowing Devon would scratch her stomach.

Pat shook his head. He didn't think his dog even greeted *him* that affectionately, but then Devon inspired that kind of adoration. It was impossible to know her and not be fueled by her enthusiasm for life. Whether it be work or play, Devon was usually surrounded by a group of laughing, loyal people.

"All right, monster," she said, giving the dog one final pat. "I have other things to do besides rub your tummy."

The dog whined and leaped up again, begging to differ that anything could be more important. Bending down to restrain the dog, Pat glanced at Devon's long, shapely legs. He straightened quickly. "So how was work?"

"Since it's Saturday, it was fine," she said.

"I meant this week."

"Pretty much the same as when you asked me last night." She gave him a concerned look. "Are you all right? You look kind of funny."

"That's not a very nice thing to say to my famous bachelor brother," Dan teased as he walked into the kitchen.

Leslie joined them. "If you looked funny, no one would notice," she told Dan. "But Pat doesn't usually look that way."

"Very funny," Dan retorted. "And I was just about to offer you both a cold drink." Dan poured two iced teas for the women anyway.

"We take it all back, you're a gentleman and a scholar," Devon told him with a smile.

"Devon's up to something if she just called Dan a gentleman," Pat said, grateful for the interruption.

"And a scholar," Leslie added. "It might be heat stroke."

"Fine. I know when I'm not wanted," Dan pouted in good humor. "Devon, care to join me?"

Pat watched her walk outside with his brother, noting the way her hips softly swayed. Out of the corner of his eye he saw Leslie watching him with an amused look on her face. "I better go check the grill," he told her. Pat shook his head thinking how oddly his friends and family had behaved in the past week. If one more person asked him about the fishing trip with a knowing smile, he'd pull his hair out. They must be wondering how he got along with Sunny. He found subtle ways to let everyone know Sunny was just a friend now; no danger from the curse there. Funny thing, though, that just made them smile even more. Maybe it was something in the water.

Several of those curious friends were outside, some with children, others single, and happy to be so, as they watched one mother run ragged after her three-year-old. Pat watched as Devon shook her head at the little terror's antics. She stripped down to the swimsuit she wore under her shorts and jumped into the pool.

"Come on, Tyler. I'll help you." She held her arms up for the delighted youngster. Catching the child, she began playing Mulberry Bush with him in the shallow end of Pat's pool.

As Pat watched her splash with the happily squealing child, everything else seemed to fade away. Laughing and swirling around with Tyler, she helped him float and blow bubbles. The boy's mother sent Devon a grateful look and sank into a chair to enjoy the respite. Pat always marveled at how wonderful Devon was with kids. This was a woman who could calmly wrangle millions of dollars from corporations for old buildings and stand before the legislature charming them into more money for museums. Yet she'd always had a way with children, making them feel important and special. More kids joined her as the shallow end of the pool became a "Let's dunk Devon" arena.

Suddenly, he realized he wasn't the only one watching her. Several of his single friends were giving her the same admiring looks they always gave her. Pat told himself he shouldn't blame them. She was beautiful. He had watched most of his friends since college make fools of themselves trying to woo her. But really, there were Bob and Jeff, both practically drooling over her and they knew she wasn't interested. Bob's eyes glazed over at the mention of historical homes and Pat had long since warned Devon about Jeff's reputation with women. Even Michael couldn't take his eyes off her, and Pat specifically remembered telling him Devon visited pioneer cemeteries for fun so there was absolutely no excuse for the charming grin he was now giving her.

He took a deep breath and reminded himself that Devon, of all people, could take care of herself and he couldn't blame the guys. She truly was lovely and there was something about her today that was especially eye-catching. Maybe it was the swimsuit. He had seen Devon in swimsuits a hundred times, from the truly awful green one in seventh grade to her first bikini two years later. He had spent that summer giving killer looks to the drooling teenage boys that suddenly appeared in her parents' backyard every Saturday. Back then he never noticed how stunning she looked in one though. He wondered when he had begun to notice. Probably about the time she grew those beautiful, long legs. As she jumped out of the pool to chase Tyler, Pat took in the curves and golden skin. Some suit.

She captured the boy and swung him into the air as sunlight filtered over her, making her sparkle and dance before his eyes. Watching her, Pat swallowed the aching lump in his throat. It was the same feeling he had at the cabin when he held her. His heart felt as though it had outgrown his chest while a sweet warmth spread through him.

Devon. Wonderful, beautiful, zany Devon. He had a sinking feeling he knew just what this feeling was. Love. Not the "I'll always be your friend" kind, but the "I want to be with you forever" kind. Devon. Of course it would be Devon. Who was his favorite person to spend time with? Who did he call when something good or bad happened? Who else did he trust with his hopes and dreams? Devon. He could feel a ridiculous smile growing as he watched her. He loved her. For the first time in his life he felt like doing something crazy, like dancing a jig or shouting this wonderful news at the top of his lungs.

No, he probably shouldn't do that. Devon appreciated spontaneity as much as anyone, but this was a much more delicate matter. He had begun to recognize this feeling last Christmas and casually mentioned he was thinking about settling down. The next day she suggested him as the next McKenzie Man to Eugenia. He thought that was clear enough at the time and tried to keep things in perspective these past few months. Lately though, he was less and less satisfied with being just friends.

Past mishaps aside, he knew in this moment that she was the perfect woman for him. He thought she had been just as affected by their time together last week at the cabin. Of course, knowing Devon, it was not going to be easy convincing her how wonderful it really was. This would take finesse, strategy, and infinite patience. He snapped out of his reverie when he saw Dan staring at him. His brother was wearing an exceptionally delighted expression for a man who was burning the burgers.

"Hey! Watch the grill," he called. Dan dove for the burgers and Pat grabbed a plate to catch the well-done meat that came flying his way.

"That one's Devon's. She likes them burnt."

"I'll cook Devon's," Pat told him. "You never get it right."

Dan gave him the meat tongs. "Devon looks great, don't you think?" he asked.

Pat pulled himself together to look at his brother. "Yes, beautiful." He scowled as his brother grinned like an idiot, then walked away to join Devon.

She stood in front of a backdrop of flowers, talking to friends. Pat felt incredibly poetic for a moment, thinking she was like a rose—beautiful, sweet-smelling to those who stopped to savor her, and yet strong enough to survive a harsh winter. Of course, there were just enough thorns thrown in to make you appreciate the other qualities, he thought with a grin.

His amusement faded as he realized one of his best friends seemed to be admiring those other qualities a bit too closely. Pat handed the tongs to a startled passerby and headed for Mitch, carefully repeating Oregon's penal code for manslaughter.

Devon laughed at one of Mitch's outrageous jokes when she looked up to see Pat stalking toward them. He had a thunderous look on his face. She shot an alarmed look to Dan, but he just crossed his arms and grinned at her as Pat approached.

"I thought you might be getting cold," Pat said, handing Devon an oversized T-shirt.

"Thank you," she told him and accepted the shirt with some confusion. It was nearly ninety degrees and she couldn't imagine why Pat would think she was cold. He was probably just being courteous, she thought and blotted off some of the water from the pool. She laid the shirt on a nearby chair.

"It's really beautiful today," she assured him. "Nice and warm, don't you think?" Pat walked away shaking his head. "Did Pat just *growl?*" she asked, bewildered. From the corner of her eye she saw Dan and Mitch high-fiving.

"Yes," Leslie said, laughing. "I think you could call it that."

Devon looked suspiciously at the three of them while they stood, grinning at some private joke. "What have you done?"

"It's not what *we've* done," Dan told her cryptically, kissing her forehead.

As the boys followed Pat, Devon shook her head. "They're acting really weird."

"They're men. They always act weird," Leslie said.

"This is more weird than usual," Devon said. "I'm going to check on the food."

When Oregon had great weather, it really had it, Devon thought an hour later, finally relaxing in an over-sized hammock. She had mingled with friends, eaten a perfectly cooked burger—courtesy of Pat—and now she stretched out under the shade of an enormous black walnut tree and relaxed. She had missed Oregon's temperate climate during her college years at the

University of Arizona. For someone born and bred in the drizzly mists of Eugene, she thought she was going to die when Tucson hit 110 degrees.

Things were perfect now that she was back home. She had the perfect job and the perfect life. She glanced around the half-acre backyard, filled with old friends and new. Dorky was sneaking up on Mitch's plate, taking advantage of his lack of attention. Tyler was now running his father ragged, refusing to take a nap, but desperately needing one. Someone searched for the water volleyball and Devon sipped her tea while the sounds of children laughing and grown-ups playing surrounded the peaceful setting. In the pool, Sunny was in the process of trying to drown Dan; obviously a woman of discerning taste, Devon thought, chuckling as Dan came up sputtering. In the nature of good sportsmanship she had invited Sunny herself. Now that the beautiful blond was no longer a threat to Pat's peace of mind, Devon had to admit that she actually liked Sunny.

Pat's deep laughter carried across the yard from where he stood on the patio, talking with colleagues. From the haven of her sunglasses, Devon watched him. Several rounds of golf this summer had bronzed his skin a golden tan and despite his brother's teasing he had a great physique. A Seahawk's baseball cap covered his dark head, making him look boyish and relaxed. This wasn't really the first time she had noticed how attractive Pat was. It was hard not to notice when someone invokes such a dramatic response in the female of the species. Even before becoming the McKenzie Man, Pat had attracted women of all sorts with his good looks and gentle temperament.

Devon had been largely immune to his charms however. Until that summer after her freshman year in college. After being away for nine months, she had returned home and stood tongue-tied before the gorgeous man who came to dinner at her parent's house. It was as though she had always kept the picture of her childhood friend in place, then after the long absence, made a shocking discovery. Pat had grown up, and rather nicely, too. After several uncomfortable encounters, where she tried to control her quivering nerves whenever he walked into a room, he had done the unthinkable. He had introduced her to his girlfriend.

In a blazingly brilliant move she had spent the evening flirting with Dan to assuage her bruised heart. The sparks that had always been there flamed easily. Throwing herself into that newfound territory with the enthusiasm she gave everything, Devon had kept busy, ignoring Pat and proving to herself she was not attracted to him. Instead, she and Dan had been inseparable for three weeks. Until the night at Slide Rock. Devon shook her head at that disastrous memory. It was enough to convince her that Dan and Pat were meant to be big brothers, nothing more.

Now, Pat stripped off his shirt and dived into the pool, capturing the volleyball. Dan startled Devon out of her reverie, scooping her into his arms. "Ready to play?" he teased, then dumped her in the deep end beside Pat.

She came up gasping, pushing the heavy hair from her face. "Stinking twerp," she muttered.

"Excuse me?" Pat asked in amusement.

"Not you," she explained. "Your little brother." Pat nodded as he had a hundred times before and tossed the ball to the other side. Devon marveled at the change in Pat as he served the ball. Ninety percent of the time, Pat was the most mild-mannered, constant man she knew, next to her father. Then, he joined in a competitive sport and it was like watching a transformation. Something in his eyes said he was not going to lose, no matter how tough the challenge. It was the reason Devon always joined his team. Unfortunately, it also meant she would be playfully bowled over several times a game by a man who would not accept defeat.

Normally Devon would be equally aggressive, running Pat over and ribbing him when they collided, but this time she had trouble concentrating on the game. The first time Pat dove for the ball, he took them both under. Strong arms pulled her back to the surface and as she gasped for air, Pat's laughing face hovered inches from her, his eyes sparkling with fun. For some reason Devon couldn't breathe. Maybe she should have waited longer after eating?

"Your serve," he said, handing her the ball.

Devon served the ball and tried to concentrate on anything but the memory of his sleek body holding hers. She was almost grateful when Dorky decided to join the game. Unfortunately the dog got in the way and helped Dan's team score a point, which made Pat banish her from the pool. The dripping, broken-hearted canine responded by showering her owner with a cascade of water when she shook off. The good-natured ribbing from both sides continued while Devon made every effort to pay attention. It wasn't easy when she couldn't take her eyes off the extremely healthy male body next to her.

She was losing her mind. That must be why she couldn't remember ever seeing a man look so good in a swimsuit. She scowled and mentally chided herself. Pat had made it clear years ago that they were just friends. She would never again risk that precious friendship with a schoolgirl crush, she told herself firmly, so she should just keep her mind on the game and stop drooling.

"Look out!"

Devon ducked instinctively as the ball splashed down in front of her. Dorky barked madly and leaped in, nearly drowning Pat in her haste to rescue Devon. In the mayhem, Devon blushed furiously at Pat's questioning look.

"Where were you?" he asked in a teasing voice.

"Somewhere I shouldn't be," she muttered. "I think I'll go entertain your dog for awhile. Come on, Dorky!"

Pat pushed the dog out of the pool, ducking underwater to avoid the shower this time.

"Was it something we said?" Dan called.

"I'm just going to see if you ate all the food," she called back and fled to the patio, wondering what it would take to get Pat out of her head this time.

"This is great," Sunny said as Devon poured herself an ice water. Sunny stood holding a brownie in one hand and a diet soda in the other. She grinned at Devon's look. "This way I don't feel quite as guilty."

"They're going to kill themselves," Leslie announced, joining them. "Pat scored a great shot and now Dan and Mitch are trying to out-do it."

"Are they always so competitive?" Sunny asked.

Leslie and Devon looked at each other and nodded in unison. "Always."

"By the way, how did you get away from Dan?" Leslie asked. "He's been your shadow all afternoon."

Sunny shrugged. "He hasn't been that bad."

Devon laughed. "Oh no," she said in an exaggerated voice. "And he hasn't been looking at you every three seconds either," she teased. "This is the only time I've ever seen him pay attention to anything but the game."

Sunny blushed. "You're exaggerating."

"Wanna bet?" Devon asked.

"Sure."

"I'll bet he looks over here before the next serve," Devon told her.

Sunny started to answer, then shook her head as they watched the pool. Devon burst out laughing as Dan looked to Sunny and waved, missing the serve that landed in front of him.

"What do I lose?"

"I don't know. I'll think of something though," Devon promised in an evil voice.

"You're one to talk," Sunny retorted. "I noticed you had a little trouble concentrating on the game."

"At least Pat is just as bad," Leslie added, wiggling her eyebrows at Devon before leaving to watch the game.

"No, he's not," Devon said, then blushed, realizing she had just admitted *she* was that bad.

"I bet he looks over here before the next serve," Sunny said.

"What are we betting?"

Sunny thought for a moment. "Information," she finally decided.

"About Pat?" Devon asked cautiously. She could have sworn Sunny wasn't interested, but with that stupid curse lurking around, nothing made sense.

"No, about Dan," Sunny said.

"No problem. You're on."

The words were no sooner out of her mouth than Pat glanced her way, smiling at her an instant before the ball was served. Devon sighed. Apparently she could add predictable to the Lawrence brothers' other qualities. "What do you want to know?"

"What happened between you and Dan in college?"

Devon choked on an ice cube in her water. "Dan told you about that?"

"No. A little bird told me," Sunny said with a grin.

"Hmmm." Devon thought madly for a distraction. "Have another brownie," she offered.

"Come on, a deal's a deal," Sunny goaded her.

Devon shrugged as they walked toward some comfortable chairs away from the crowd. "We just realized we were meant to be friends."

"How?"

Devon sighed in frustration. She might as well get it over with. "We went up to Slide Rock and spent the day playing in the river. That night we were getting ready to leave . . ."

"And?"

"And it was really beautiful and romantic," she admitted, smiling now at the memory.

"And?"

"We kissed," Devon told her.

"And?"

"That was it."

"That was it? You were in the middle of paradise with a gorgeous man and that was it?"

"Uh-huh."

"How come?" Sunny asked as she watched the game end in the pool. Pat's team won and Dan was receiving his share of friendly abuse.

Devon shook her head at the memory of that moonlit night. "Because it felt like kissing my brother. Too weird. We just sat there looking at each other and realized we both felt the same way. Anyhow, we came home and have been friends ever since."

"No regrets?" Sunny asked.

"Dan and I would have killed each other if we had gotten any more serious. We're just too much alike."

Sunny nodded thoughtfully. "Not like Pat," she said casually.

"Really nice weather we're having."

"Now kissing him probably wouldn't be like kissing somebody's brother," Sunny added.

"I've heard this has been a banner year for vegetables."

Sunny laughed in response, raising her glass in a salute as she took the hint.

"Hey! What are you two doing? Hiding?" Dan asked as he joined them.

"No. Sunny was just being annoying," Devon gave her a pointed look that didn't shame her companion a bit.

"Be careful or she'll sic Charlie on you," Dan told Sunny.

"Who's Charlie?"

"Her cat," Dan said with a perfectly straight face.

"And this is supposed to be scary?" Sunny scoffed.

"Ask Pat. The cat hates him," Dan said.

"Charlie doesn't hate Pat. I think he actually likes him," Devon defended her pet.

"That's why he leaves paw prints all over his clean car and hairballs on anything Pat leaves at your house?" Dan asked.

"Yes. Most people he ignores," Devon explained.

"Lucky Pat," Sunny murmured.

"Why am I so lucky?" Pat asked joining them.

"We were talking about how much Charlie loves you," Dan told him.

"Wretched animal," Pat muttered with as much animosity as anyone would ever see from him.

Dan winked at Devon as they both had heard Pat grumbling about Charlie for nearly twenty years. Pat had rescued the ragged, starving kitten from some boys who had tied firecrackers to its tail. In gratitude, the little ball of scruff had bitten him before climbing into Devon's arms and purring happily. She often wondered if Charlie wasn't simply jealous of Pat. Charlie certainly made his feelings clear, she thought, especially the time he caught that garden snake and left it on the driver's seat of Pat's car. She could have sworn the little fiend was smiling when Pat rather excitedly exited the vehicle.

Pat grimaced at the mention of the dreaded feline. "He pushes my buttons just because he knows I can't kill him."

"He'd come back to haunt you," Devon said with a grin.

"At least he wouldn't be able to sharpen his claws on my tires then," Pat reminded her. He started to ruffle Devon's hair, then stopped, an odd look on his face. Instead, he tucked a wayward curl behind her ear and headed back to the pool.

Then Dan ruffled her hair with a delighted grin and followed his brother. Devon gave Sunny a bemused look. "Do you think they've been in the sun too long?" she asked.

Sunny laughed. "Maybe."

Chapter Seven

"Where are the boys?" Devon asked. She glanced around the party while cleaning up and realized with some chagrin that all the men had disappeared. She was not about to tackle the grill, so she had been looking surreptitiously for Pat for twenty minutes. It certainly wasn't because she was actually *looking* for him.

"Where do you think?" Leslie said and glanced to the top of the house.

"Of course." Devon was surprised it had taken them this long. Pat's model train set in the attic was a magnet to every adult male who had ever entered the house.

She finished cleaning up and said good-bye to a few friends who were leaving. Tyler mumbled a sleepy good-bye and gave her a sticky kiss before falling asleep again on his father's shoulder. Leslie and Sunny

93

joined the remaining women in lounge chairs around the pool. Time to relax and enjoy the last bit of summer warmth. As Devon walked through the house, she noted even Dorky had succumbed to an afternoon nap, sprawled in front of Pat's favorite chair. After the number of hamburgers Dorky had gotten away with, Devon wasn't surprised. She could do with a nap herself, she thought as she started slowly up the stairs.

Devon remembered when Pat had first seen the house. Trying to be diplomatic about the disaster, he had declared the attic would be perfect for his model train set. She tried to convince him to put the monstrosity in the basement but he had been firm. Since it was the only thing he felt strongly about, and considering the condition of the battered old house, she decided it best not to press her luck. The train had gone in the attic and now men of all ages beat a path up two flights of stairs to see it. She climbed the first set of stairs, her hand caressing the rich pine bannister as she went. The steps still gleamed from the refinishing she had done last spring. The rich, honey-toned wood made the old house feel warm and alive. As she started up the second set of stairs to the attic, she could hear the voices. She could envision the guys, scattered around the train set, probably gossiping just like their wives downstairs.

"You don't know how good you have it, Pat," one male voice announced.

"Enjoy your bachelor days while you can," another added.

"You've got a great job, great life, and an incredible house. Why mess it up?"

"Yeah. What if you meet somebody and she hates this house?"

"What?" Pat's startled reply muffled Devon's own gasp.

"Some women would think this place is just a lot of work. I mean, my wife wanted a new house or nothing at all. There's no way she'd live in an old house."

Devon leaned against the wall, astonished. This was Pat's house. She couldn't imagine him living anywhere else.

"I can't imagine living anywhere else," he echoed her thoughts out loud.

Dan laughed. "That's not what you thought when Devon showed it to you the first time."

Mitch snorted. "You thought it was a dump. But you didn't want to hurt Devon's feelings because she was so wild about it."

"Yeah, but the girl knows her stuff," another voice added. "You could sell it and make a killing."

Devon pressed a hand over her heart.

"I have no intention of selling. This is my home. I like it here."

"Mark my words. You'll meet some beautiful babe and the next thing you know, you're at the country club and this place has a 'For Sale' sign in front."

"I guess I'll just have to make sure I marry someone who loves this place," Pat's thoughtful voice responded.

"Man, Devon would kill you if you ever sold this place."

"You could sell it to her. It's practically hers anyway," Dan offered.

"I don't think I would sell it to Devon," Pat said softly.

"With the amount of work she's put in it, at least you should split the profit," Mitch offered helpfully.

"No," Pat said. "I think I have a better idea. Anyone want a soda?"

Devon silently flew down the stairs, ducking into the master bedroom. With a hand over her pounding heart, she waited quietly until Pat had passed on his way to the kitchen. She sat on the king-sized, custom-built sleigh bed and tried to breathe. From the moment she had seen this house it had said "Pat" to her. She had never considered that he might not always live here. Or that he would marry someone who didn't want it.

Why wouldn't someone want it? she thought, getting angry now. She designed it to grow with a family. It had been a farmhouse to a large family to begin with. She had also accommodated all of Pat's needs—the train, the whirlpool, and the big-screen TV—while keeping the sanctity of the house. A woman would be out of her mind to not love it.

But what about the work? her conscience reminded her. She may think spending summers and weekends rebuilding an antique monstrosity fun, but most women would probably be terrified by the prospect. She glanced around the master bedroom and saw beauty everywhere. From the lead-glass picture window to the hand-restored cabinet that hid a television and VCR, it was beautiful, yet functional. Even the master bath with its antique water spouts that somehow looked right at home in the marbled whirlpool bath, it was all comfortable yet classic. Sort of like the home's owner.

She ran a hand over the bed's footrail and for the first time thought of the woman who might someday share this bed for a lifetime. She could feel the color drain out of her face as she realized it was something she had never really thought out. She picked out the bed, thinking it'd be a great place to read bedtime stories, a sturdy bed that would survive a few hundred pillow fights and tickling matches. *With someone else's children.* For a single, shocking moment Devon realized what she had done. She hadn't designed the house for Pat. She'd designed it for herself. And Pat. Somewhere, lurking in the depths of her subconscious, she had been building her own nest.

"Hi. Everything okay?" Pat asked from the doorway. He took one look at her and put the six-pack of sodas down, closing the door. "Honey, what's the matter?"

She looked at him, wondering if she had ever seen him before. He looked so perfectly natural here in this house. They both were built to last, she thought. The man and the house had character, beauty, and staying power. Those qualities were why she loved the house. They were also the reasons why she loved Pat. Good grief. She loved Pat. She felt her heart hammer in her chest and wondered if it would help if she put her head between her knees. No, she thought ruefully. There wasn't going to be an easy cure for this. She was honestly, truly in love with the latest McKenzie Man. Unfortunately he was also her best friend. Wetting her dry lips with her tongue she tried to answer. "I was just thinking."

"About what?" Pat sat next to her as he had a hundred times before and wrapped his arms around her. When she sat stiffly in their warm circle, he pulled her down to the bed, cradling her on his chest. Devon tried to steady her breath as she felt his warmth surrounding her. A multitude of confusing feelings whirled through her, not the least being a fierce wanting for the man who lay beside her.

She rested her cheek on his chest and tried to relax, listening to his heart beating, steady and strong. Pat's fingers massaged her cold and tense ones while he quietly held her, waiting for her to tell him all her problems. Except this time, *he* was her problem. What could she say? *Marry me.* The thought leaped from nowhere and nearly strangled her. She pushed away from his warmth and shot from the bed. For a moment she wondered if she had spoken the words out loud. He looked at her in surprise.

"Devi? Did I do something wrong?"

"No," she shook her head. "I just remembered something downstairs." Turning, she fled down the stairs to the sunlight and sanity.

Chapter Eight

A rainy Sunday. In Oregon. Imagine that, Devon thought grimly, as she stood in her kitchen. After all the activity at the party yesterday, she probably should rest, but instead, she felt restless, and in a rainstorm, her choices were limited. She spent the morning mentally reiterating that everything was fine with Pat. Just because she had trouble breathing around him lately, this was not an insurmountable problem. She could and would put this behind her. As much as she enjoyed a little chaos in her life, she did not appreciate it in her relationship with Pat. Pat was a sane harbor and nothing, not a full moon, nor out-of-control hormones, would ruin that.

Having firmly admonished herself, she looked around for something to keep busy. For a woman who relished ripping out walls and replacing them, she wasn't in a creative or even destructive mood. Besides, she liked her home the way it was, with the walls intact. She could cook something, but then she'd have to eat it herself. She could call a girlfriend and go to a movie, but she didn't think she could sit still that long. Charlie wrapped himself around her ankles, purring. She picked him up and stroked his fur. "You really are huge, bud. Are you ready to go on that diet Doc James says you need?"

"Mrowr!"

She rubbed his ears. "I didn't think so." She buried her face in his soft fur. She had just fed him and he was limp with gratitude. "You do have it made," she told him. Even though it had been nearly twenty years since Pat rescued that starving, scruffy little kitten, Charlie still worried over his food bowl. She didn't have the heart to put him on a diet when he kept a daily check on his food bag. He could tell when it was getting low and acted worried until the new bag came in. She put him on his favorite blanket on the window seat over the heater. He stretched, curled into a sizeable ball and promptly fell asleep.

She should probably eat herself, but she didn't feel like eating with her stomach doing flip flops. Maybe she could cook something for someone else to eat. She thought about it. Of course. She could make something to share with her best friend. She did that all the time, she reminded herself. So why did her heart skip a beat at the thought of spending the afternoon with him? No, this would be an excellent opportunity to prove to herself that she could be a responsible adult where a certain tall, dark-haired man was concerned. It was just a meal, like a thousand others they had shared over the years. Nothing to feel queasy about. *Right,* she thought, rubbing her stomach. *No big deal.*

The idea formed and percolated in her brain. In minutes she had the items she needed and called Pat. No answer. He was probably playing basketball with the boys. She could surprise him with homemade soup and fresh bread. It's a good thing she had forced him to buy that bread machine. She couldn't remember all the times they enjoyed the smell of something wonderful cooking in his crock pot. This would be just a normal thing. So why didn't anything feel normal with Pat anymore?

As she was about to put her key in the lock to his house, she stopped, feeling awkward about entering his home. She took a deep breath and leaned her forehead against the burnished walnut door. She had used her keys countless times before, just as Pat had used his keys to her house. It wasn't like she was going to barge in on him with a hot date. For some reason, that thought made her feel terrible. No, she reasoned, not when she was most likely to be the woman in his arms lately. For some reason that made her smile.

Greeting Dorky, she brought in the supplies, washed up, and went to work. It didn't take long before the hearty vegetable soup was cooking. Sometimes it seemed like she had cooked more meals in Pat's kitchen than her own. It was probably true. She loved his kitchen—she *had* designed it—so it only made sense she spent so much time here. As the bread machine began whirling, she stepped back, savoring the sense of satisfaction. In a couple hours the kitchen would be filled with a wonderful aroma, just the way a house like this should smell. Now that the spurt of activity was finished though, she felt restless again.

She could read. Pat probably had some riveting law manuals lying around. She could watch a movie, but looking over his video collection, she wasn't in the mood for an old western and a romantic comedy was definitely out of the question. Why couldn't he be like other guys and have some great action movies? That would safely burn off some of this restless energy, she thought. Dorky whined, seeming to understand her mood. At least Pat had a couple of CDs that she had left there. Within minutes the sounds of Mozart filled the house.

Walking into the living room, Devon ran her hands over the fireplace mantel. She had spent an entire summer stripping the mantel and ceiling cornices. Under the years of dirt and layers of paint around the fireplace, she had found the treasure she was looking for. Antique cherry wood gleamed now, with delicate pineapple carvings that were so popular with Victorian architects. The pineapples symbolized hospitality, and Devon loved that just as she loved entertaining here. She couldn't count the number of times friends and family gathered here just to relax and enjoy each other.

That was part of what she loved about old houses. They reminded her of a time when people played cards and talked instead of watching television.

Still, she couldn't remember ever feeling quite so restless here. She had been working sporadically with Dan and Pat to remodel the basement and could certainly spend a few hours down there. The smallest bedroom upstairs needed paint, wallpaper, and new light fixtures, all waiting for her in a tidy box in the corner. For some reason, she just couldn't concentrate enough to really start such a large project. She wandered back to the kitchen, aimlessly looking through the refrigerator and freezer. Suddenly she spied the answer. Huckleberries. There in the freezer was a container of the ill-fated little treats. Her mouth watered at the thought of huckleberry shortcake.

Rummaging through Pat's pantry, she found all she needed. After digging up a recipe, Devon thawed the berries in a pan of hot water. She measured the dry ingredients, then reached for the tub of berries. The lid stuck as she tried to pry it open. In exasperation, Devon yanked on the lid and then watched in amazement as a ghastly purple stain spread over her favorite white shirt. Most of the berries graciously landed back in the bowl, but they left a tie-dyed trail over her cotton blouse.

Devon realized she needed to wash it immediately. Quickly stripping it off, she wadded it up gingerly and walked to the back bathroom. One of the inconveniences of buying a home that was built before modern plumbing was the lack of foresight in said plumbing.

When Pat bought the home, the dank basement housed some haphazard hookups for a washer and dryer. Claiming it wasn't up to code, Pat had improvised, while Devon teased him about being afraid of the dark.

He'd installed a small, stackable laundry unit in the back bathroom. The tiny room now housed a minuscule shower stall, a pedestal sink, a commode, and the laundry. The set-up worked, but left no room for storage. Pat solved that by stacking his laundry detergents on top of the dryer, which was no problem if you're six-foot-two. Devon reached on tiptoe for stain remover, and after rinsing it as best she could, she threw the shirt in the washer and pulled down the box of detergent. She quickly threw a cupful in and pushed the detergent back on top. Unfortunately, she didn't quite get it all the way on top before she let go. As the box fell, sticky white powder cascaded over her like a fluffy ocean wave. Devon sputtered and shook and watched in amazement as the soap covered her feet in a soft mound.

Slowly she counted backwards. This was Pat's fault. If he didn't have the stupid huckleberries; if he hadn't gotten hurt getting them; if he hadn't put the laundry in the small bathroom; if he hadn't made her fall in love with him—none of this would have happened. She wanted to cry, but the way things were going, she'd probably end up in suds to her ears, floating through the house like Alice in Wonderland. Taking a deep breath, she graciously decided the soap wasn't his fault, even if everything else was. After painstakingly cleaning the biggest portion of the mess up, she stuffed the bathroom rug into the laundry with her shirt and socks. At least she wouldn't need to add any more detergent, she thought grimly, shaking herself to get rid of the white powder that still clung to her. Then she carefully swept the floor and toweled up the remaining bits of white. The floor felt sticky so she quickly ran a mop over it, then hoped the entire mess would dry before Pat came home.

Pat. He could be home any minute and she was gallivanting about his house in bra and bare feet. That would certainly match the rest of her behavior lately. It should also send the latest McKenzie Man fleeing for the hills and this time he wouldn't invite her along. Devon grimly headed up the stairs to his room and vowed she would shoot the next person who mentioned huckleberries to her.

Pat just wanted a warm Jacuzzi and cold beer when he got home. He was too old for this he thought, flexing his sore back and shoulders. Either that or he and Mitch would have to stay off the topic of Devon. Halfway through their basketball game Mitch had mentioned how he'd always wanted to ask Devon out and would Pat mind? Trying really hard not to pulverize his old and dear friend, he had carefully explained all of Devon's failings. She was willful and stubborn and she tended to leap before she looked. And opinionated? He had never seen such an opinionated woman. She really was a handful. He had stopped halfway through his litany when his "friends" had collapsed on the court in laughter.

So much for subtlety, he thought. Then he forgot everything as he pulled into the driveway and saw Devon's car. How many days had he enjoyed that, working with her on one of their houses, something incredible cooking in the kitchen? In a considerably lighter frame of mind, he opened the door softly, putting his bag on the floor. Pandora trotted to him, tail wagging in delight. Quietly rubbing her ears, he watched Devon working in the kitchen. The dog rejoined her as she mixed some batter and poured it into a pan. Pat propped a shoulder against the door frame, wishing he could capture this moment forever. For some reason she was wearing one of his shirts, the rounded shirttail covering her hips. Even with the sleeves rolled up several times, she had to push them up occasionally.

A wisp of hair escaped her ponytail and Pat had to stop himself from reaching out to push it back. Pink toenails peaked out from under her jeans as she put the pan in the oven. She looked perfect, Pat thought as his exhausted senses responded to her nearness. Finesse and patience, he reminded himself. That strategy probably left out attacking her in his kitchen just because she looked adorable. The dog and lady fell into a well-rehearsed dance as Devon walked to a cupboard and Pandora moved out of the way only enough to keep from being stepped on. They were comfortable together here in his house. Their house, his mind corrected. If anything, Devon put more work into his house than her own. Although hers was a beautifully restored 1908 cottage, he knew his house truly reflected all of her talent and love for the historical.

It also reflected her love for him, he thought. She was as dedicated to the people in her intimate circle of relationships as she was to restoring old houses. Having her priorities straight had never been a problem for Devon. She glowed with passion for life and the people she loved. He remembered when she and Dan helped him rip out ancient kitchen cupboards and replace them with custom cabinets with lead glass panels. Another time, Dan teased him when he admitted he liked those little blue flowers in Leslie's yard. Devon appeared the next weekend with enamel doorknobs painted with delicate cornflowers. The flowers also appeared in tasteful stencils and patterns in the kitchen, but somehow Devon still made the affair masculine with dark blue plaid prints and simple, state-of-the-art appliances. That was one of Devon's gifts. She took the time to learn what other people's interests and tastes were, then incorporated them into something that made sense.

No one knew him as well as Devon, he realized. Like the big screen TV that somehow worked in the family room alongside windows and lights that would have looked right here a hundred years ago. He never had to tell her he wanted one. She simply took him shopping while he enthused about all the latest electronic gadgets. He remembered she was looking a little cross-eyed by the time he settled on his choice. Within weeks the room was finished and ready for the monstrosity and somehow it looked like it was made for the place.

That was like Devon. All the energy and passion and contradictions somehow jelled to make her the most amazing woman he knew. Kind, generous, and hot-tempered, he couldn't remember her ever doing something mean-spirited, no matter how much she was provoked. He rubbed his chest and knew the ache wasn't from playing too hard. He wanted to share every aspect of her life. He wanted to be more than just best friends. He wanted to be lovers and parents and meddling grandparents together. He wanted to be with her for the rest of his life.

He loved planning a strategy for the courtroom, maybe he just needed to have a strategy for this. If he could get past the rush of emotion clogging his senses he could devise a plan to convince her something was missing in this house. It was missing her.

Lifting the lid on the crock pot, Devon inhaled the wonderful aroma. The smell enveloped the kitchen making Dorky whine. "Patience, girl. It's not ready till your master gets home." Dorky whined again and trotted to the door. Devon jumped a foot as she saw Pat leaning against the door jamb. He grinned at her while she tried to slow her racing heart.

"Sorry," he said. "I didn't mean to startle you. You just looked so incredibly beautiful, I couldn't help but watch."

Devon's jaw dropped open then snapped shut. Beautiful? Pat? Maybe he had hit his head. She really wished the guys wouldn't play so hard. It was a miracle they didn't kill each other in their "friendly" game. He looked okay, though, except for that goofy grin on his face. He looked great, actually. Amazing how the right man can make a sweaty T-shirt and shorts look sexy. He walked to the crock pot and inhaled. "That smells incredible. What is it?"

"What?" she asked as her brain tried to grasp anything but the wonderful smell of him standing inches from her.

"The food. What is it?"

"Soup. It's just soup," she stammered. His hair was still damp with sweat and he had that flushed, "just been playing" look that made his skin glow. If she were an artist, this is how she would paint him, she thought haphazardly before stepping back.

"I made bread and soup. No big deal." She glanced at her watch. "I better be going."

"Going?" he asked sharply. "Why don't you stay?"

"I have a ton of stuff to do and you need a shower," she said.

"Sorry," Pat said softly.

"Don't be," Devon whispered. If she didn't leave now, she was going to throw herself, and all of her careful resolutions at him. With a pounding heart she looked around for her keys.

Pat caught her arm. "Please don't go."

"I have to," she murmured.

The next instant she realized he was going to kiss her and she couldn't have stopped it if she wanted to. Then all rational thought fled as his lips covered hers. Devon relaxed in his arms as she met the kiss. If this was wrong, why did her body feel like it had discovered an oasis in the desert? Completely against her will, her hands ran under his shirt, feeling the soft hair on his chest, marveling in the way his body flexed at her touch. The quietness of the man belied his strength. He felt solid as a rock and so completely right. He gently ran his lips over hers, ever so slowly and sweetly. Devon sighed in surrender as his hands roamed over her back, deepening the embrace. He nuzzled her neck, his lips softly caressing the sensitive skin there. Giving her a tender look, he sniffed her hair. "You smell good. Like clean laundry."

Devon could feel herself blushing. "I really have to go," she said softly, desperately trying to keep from throwing him on the floor and having her way with him. This was *Pat* for heaven's sake. She took an unsteady step back.

"Please stay. I promise to be good," he teased.

Devon gave him a suspicious look. How come she had never noticed how charming he could be when he was flirting? And was Pat *flirting* with her? His sexy smile made her toes curl and she wasn't even thinking about the feel of his hot and damp body next to hers. If she was going to get out of here without both of them being embarrassed she was going to have to leave now.

Fortunately, the doorbell chimed at that moment. Pat blew a frustrated sigh. He walked to the door and opened it to find a woman standing on his porch.

"Hi," she said smiling. Devon recognized the look on her face before Pat did. "I just moved to the neighborhood and heard we have a celebrity among us."

Pat stood there speechless as this was the first one that had shown up on his doorstep. 'Hello?" he said, looking completely dumbfounded. Devon blew an exasperated sigh. You would think he would be used to this by now, she thought. She picked up her car keys and tried to walk past Pat.

He caught her arm and gave her a pleading look. "I have company," he told the woman. She looked at Devon and shrugged. "Okay, I'll see you around the neighborhood." Pat shut the door and leaned his head against it.

Devon was halfway to the back door before he caught up to her. "Honey, wait."

"The timer is set for the cake and the bread will beep when it's done. The huckleberries can just be poured on top. On top of the cake, not the bread," she stammered, opening the door. "I'll see you later."

In frustration Pat watched her bolt from his house,

shoes in hand. Real finesse, he told himself in disgust. To top it off, now he needed a *cold* shower. As he tossed his gym bag in the laundry, he noticed the washing machine running. Walking upstairs, he wondered why Devon would clean his bathroom.

Chapter Nine

"Hey, Dev. Fed your face yet?"

Devon looked from the mountain of paperwork on her desk to Dan's cheerful face.

"No," she told him testily. "And some of us prefer to dine rather than feed our faces."

Dan whistled. "Hormones or bad hair day?"

Devon threw an *Architectural Digest* at him. Unfortunately it was a small one and only hit him in the head. No real damage to be done there.

"Come on," he grabbed her purse, rubbing his head. "I'll even buy."

"With the amount you consume, I should say so." She shoved the paperwork into a haphazard pile and followed him. "Where are we going?"

"Onion Press."

"Great. I won't have to worry about impressing the board this afternoon. They'll all be dead from my breath."

"I'll buy you some gum," he told her.

They walked the two blocks to the little restaurant with small booths, European decor, and a menu that featured anything that could be cooked with onions. Dan ordered a garlic and onion burger while Devon ordered her favorite, a roast beef sandwich with garlic and grilled onions.

Dan shook his head. "There's not enough gum in the world for that," he told her. "I guess it's just as well you won't be kissing anyone."

"What's that supposed to mean?"

Dan chewed his burger and tried to look innocent. It was the look that caused his mother's blood pressure to soar when they were children. "It's not like you're seeing anyone, right?" he said.

Devon opened her mouth and then closed it. No, she wasn't involved with anyone, just madly attracted to the McKenzie Man. Unfortunately he was her best friend and too nice a guy to ever tell her to back off so it'd be better to never even start down that road.

"Actually I've been thinking about it," she said.

"Oh?" Dan's eyes gleamed.

"Brad Fortune asked me out. We're having dinner together Friday," she told him. She couldn't tell him she had decided the best way to get a grip on her feelings for Pat was to focus her attention elsewhere. Maybe she would get lucky and find the man of her dreams. *Yeah, right.* That might work except the only man plaguing her dreams lately was the last man on earth she should be thinking of. She was not going to drive Pat crazy with some silly crush.

The humor left Dan's face. "No! I mean, isn't Fortune kind of old?"

"Brad's thirty-eight and owns one of the most successful software companies in the world, and besides, he's nice."

"He's a geek."

Devon laughed. "He is not. He's really attractive in an intellectual sort of way."

"He also donates a lot of money to the historical society."

"So?"

"It's a conflict of interest," Dan told her.

"In a town this size, every eligible male out there is probably a conflict of interest."

"Not necessarily," Dan said, giving his burger a moody look. "So how is Pat these days?"

Devon stopped with her sandwich inches from her mouth. "What do you mean?"

Dan shrugged and toyed with his drink. "I haven't seen much of him lately. How is he doing?"

"How should I know?" Devon told him.

"I just assumed you would have seen him since the party," Dan said.

While he waited for a reply Devon took a bite of her sandwich. "So how is work?" she finally asked.

"Fine," he told her. "Have you seen Pat since the barbeque?"

"I don't remember. I don't keep tabs on your brother."

"You two haven't had a fight have you?"

Devon gave him an exasperated look. "No. We're fine. I've been busy lately, too. How are your parents?"

"Fine." Dan polished off his burger and onion rings. "Has Pat seemed strange to you lately?"

Devon gave up. "All right, Lawrence. What do you want to know?"

"Are you in love with Pat?"

Devon swallowed hard. She couldn't lie to Dan, the wretch knew her too well, but she really didn't want to have this conversation.

"I have always loved Pat," she told him.

"You know that's not what I meant."

"Would the phrase, 'It's none of your business' mean anything to you?" Devon asked.

"Not a thing," Dan told her cheerfully.

"I admit I have noticed some of his more appealing aspects lately," she hedged.

Dan gave her a beautiful smile while she debated throwing her onion potatoes at him.

"It's about time," he told her. "Half the people on this planet think you and Pat are perfect together."

"Well, they're the half that's wrong."

"The other half just doesn't know you."

"Lucky them," Devon grumbled.

"What are you afraid of?" Dan asked.

"I'm not afraid," she said, surprised.

"I used to think you weren't afraid of anything, but now I'm not so sure. You seem pretty scared."

Devon thought about that. She had always forced herself to face her fears and move on. She never wanted to be one of those people who let life slip by because she was afraid to live it. Was Dan right? Part of what she felt holding her back was fear, a fear of losing something more precious to her than she could explain.

"This isn't like it was between us, Dev," he told her. She flinched as he seemed to read her thoughts. There was so much love in his face though that she couldn't throw something at him. Instead, she felt like crying and she never, ever felt like crying in front of Dan.

"I better get back to work," she told him. "I have a mountain of work to finish." She knew he was disappointed but she couldn't even explain her feelings to herself anymore; explaining them to Dan was out of the question.

As Dan paid the bill, Devon thought of the past two weeks and all the conflicting emotions she had felt toward Pat. How had the simplest relationship in her life become so complicated? As they walked out, Dan wrapped his arm around her, seeming to sense her mood. When they returned to her office, he stopped in the parking lot.

"I just want you to know I'm here for you if you need to talk," he told her.

"Thanks."

"And I'm in the half that knows you're perfect for Pat."

She bit her lip as she carefully studied the toe of her shoe. "I just don't know if Pat thinks so."

Dan hugged her. "Trust me," he told her. "Pat is way ahead of you on this one."

Devon shook her head, not at all convinced. He looked her in the eye. "When you kiss Pat, does it feel like kissing your brother?"

The memory of Pat's passionate embrace made her blush.

Dan smiled as he ruffled her hair. "Go get 'em, tiger."

Devon watched him walk away and wondered. Could Dan be right? There is always a first time. What if Pat felt this, too? She thought of the kiss at the cabin and again in his kitchen. It was possible. Devon shook her head. The chances of Dan being right about anything were about the same as being struck by lightning. And for once, there wasn't a cloud in the Oregon sky.

Chapter Ten

Brad Fortune had gray hair. Not really gray all over, Devon noted, but just sprinkled lightly throughout his blond hair. It was silvery and distinguished looking, but it definitely was not thick and dark and soft. His hands were nice—clean, short nails with soft, golden hair furring the backs—but his fingers weren't as long or elegant and their movements weren't nearly as graceful.

As what? She berated herself. Someone who was the last person she should be thinking of?

"Do you mind if I ask you a question?" Brad asked.

"No, go ahead," Devon told him.

"What were you just thinking of?"

Devon gave him a startled look as she wondered what her face had given away. "Why?"

"You had the most wistful look on your face, it was

really quite charming." He took a sip of wine and added, "And you were a million miles away at the time."

"I'm sorry. I guess I haven't been very good company."

"No, you've been wonderful," Brad argued. "Especially listening to me ramble about computers."

She smiled. "I had no choice. What I know about computers you could fit on the head of a pin."

"You can fit an encyclopedia on the head of a pin these days," he teased.

He really was handsome when he smiled, Devon thought. And very nice. Certainly too nice to spend the evening with a woman who was thinking of someone else.

"So, how are things at the historical society?" he asked her.

"Up to our elbows in plaster and termites," she told him, grateful to be onto a safer subject.

"And this makes you happy?" he asked, amusement lighting his features.

"I could live without the termites, but yes, it makes me happy. I'm excited about the Rosemary mansion. It could be one of the best museums of its kind if we can get all the pieces together."

"What do you need?"

"Everything," she laughed. "Right now our interior designer is trying to find antique furniture. The best pieces are either in other museums or in private collections."

"Have you thought of checking the Internet?"

"For antique furniture?" She considered this. "Morgan, our designer would probably consider it sacrilege."

"Well, if you want, I could help you design a homepage. You never know. If nothing else, it would open another avenue for free advertising."

"Something for nothing," Devon said. "I didn't think that was possible anymore."

"Anything is possible with computers," he said.

"Unless you have a complete phobia of computers. Morgan would rather mix Colonial with Art Deco than work on her computer." He looked amused by the imagery. "I'll have her call you, though. It will be good for her."

"I'll remember to take it slowly," he said with a wry grin lighting his features. Then Devon saw his eyes widen as he glanced past her shoulder. A fleeting look of terror passed over his features before he grabbed the wine menu and buried his face in it.

"Brad, are you all right?" she asked in alarm. She presumed he was when she could see the top of his head nod madly behind the menu. Oddly, several of the other men were behaving in a similar manner.

"Devon Kelly! How are you, dear?"

"Eugenia," Devon said, trying to keep a straight face as the man at the next table dropped his fork on the floor and dived under the table to retrieve it. The *McKenzie Magazine* publisher certainly had an interesting affect on single men, Devon noted with some amusement, glancing at her own dinner companion.

Eugenia Barstow pulled down the wine menu. "Hello, Brad, dear. You don't have to hide, I'm not in the market for a new McKenzie Man yet." She turned to Devon. "Or am I? Has Patrick decided to settle down yet?"

Devon shook her head as several men started ushering their dates toward the door, whether they had finished eating or not. "No, Pat is still definitely eligible."

Eugenia shook her perfectly coiffed head sadly. "What are we going to do about that?"

"We?" Devon squeaked.

The elegant woman pinned her with a look that could make strong men quiver.

Eugenia's grandfather had owned most of Eugene at one time and her late husband had made a killing on the stock market. Now Devon guessed she was somewhere in her seventies, wealthy, powerful, and apparently had too much time on her hands. It was rumored she considered the McKenzie Man some sort of mission, her own marriage having been so happy.

At the moment, she wished Eugenia would put her energy somewhere else.

"Yes, *we,* dear. After all, you were the one who thought Patrick should be married. Funny how I thought he would be my easiest match and he's still hanging on."

She paused dramatically, looking Devon over thoughtfully. "I guess some men can't see perfection even when it's right under their noses," she said, giving a careless, yet elegant shrug.

Turning to her own companion, Eugenia glanced around the rapidly emptying room with a smile. "I see I've had my usual affect on the men. We shouldn't have any trouble getting a table now."

Eugenia turned back and smiled at Brad. "Don't get too comfortable. I have high hopes Patrick won't let me down and then I'll need a new McKenzie Man."

Devon shook her head in amazement as Eugenia strolled through the restaurant, creating havoc in her wake.

Devon took in the sudden pallor on Brad Fortune's face and tried not to giggle. "I'm sure she was just teasing," she said helpfully.

"You think so?" Brad's hand shook as he drank some more wine.

Devon sighed. "Who knows if there will ever be another McKenzie Man? Pat might be a bachelor forever."

"He certainly seems to have the best of both worlds," Brad said softly.

"How do you mean?" Devon asked.

Brad blushed. "I don't want to be out of line."

"No, please." She encouraged him to speak his mind.

"I've heard you are great friends. I think it would be difficult to think of marrying when you already have one beautiful woman in your life. It's hard to have two cooks in the kitchen, so to speak."

Devon opened her mouth to reply, then closed it. Was she the reason Pat had never married? Not because he harbored some secret feelings for her, but because he just didn't need a wife when she was obviously filling the role of confidant, hostess, and, loosely speaking, companion.

"I'm sorry. I shouldn't have said anything."

She shook her head. "I think I underestimated you. I knew you were good at understanding computers, but I didn't think you could read people so well."

"One must understand people if one wants to make a computer that is easy for them to relate to."

Devon smiled. "I think some lucky woman is going to find a real prize when Eugenia picks you as the McKenzie Man."

He paled again while she tried to keep a straight face. "That's not funny," he told her.

Chapter Eleven

Devon placed the last dish in the dishwasher as the phone rang. The caller ID showed her parents' number. "Hey there," she said, knowing it was her mom's Sunday morning check-in call.

"Hello, darling. How are you?" Devon paused in the filling of the soap dispenser at the tone in her mother's voice.

"I'm fine, Mom. What's up?"

"I was wondering if you've seen the latest issue of *McKenzie Magazine*?"

"No. Did Eugenia give up on Pat and choose another McKenzie Man?"

"Well, not exactly dear."

The doorbell rang and Devon tried to close the dishwasher, wipe her hands, and hang onto the phone at once. "Mom, hang on. Someone's at the door." She still held the receiver to her ear when she opened the door to see Leslie standing there holding up the latest *McKenzie Magazine.* All coherent thought left Devon as she stared at the cover in horror.

"Oh my gosh. I'm going to murder Eugenia, Mom."

She heard the sigh on the side of the line. "I've already left a message for her. I don't care if she was best friends with my mother, she's gone too far. I told her she's off the Christmas list."

"Mom, I need to call you back. I need to have a nervous breakdown now."

Leslie took the phone from her. "Hi, Mrs. K." She paused. "Yes. Uh-huh. I brought lots of chocolate." Another pause. "I'll do that. Bye."

Leslie hung up and gave her a sympathetic look. "She said she and Mrs. Lawrence are already plotting where to hide Eugenia's body where it will never be found. She also said to remind you that you have responsibilities here and cannot leave the country."

Devon sank into a chair and stared at the color photograph of Pat standing next to her at the Eugene Historical Society ball. They were looking at each other and smiling, but that wasn't the problem. It was the huge headline: IS HE OR ISN'T HE?

She opened to the article inside with shaking hands. The magazine announced that the current McKenzie Man had been seriously involved for several months with a childhood friend and insiders said they expected an announcement of wedding bells soon. Devon felt all the blood rush from her head to her stomach and then back up again. Dizzy, she looked at Leslie.

"Hmm, maybe I didn't bring enough chocolate," her friend said.

Pat stared at the magazine cover and wished he knew a few good Irish curses to throw on Eugenia Barstow's head. The good, old-fashioned American ones he came up with didn't seem elegant enough for how much fury he felt. What in heaven's name was Eugenia thinking? The article managed to be wretched journalism, tasteless, and as ill-timed as he could imagine.

Pat rubbed his hands through his hair and wondered how Devon would react to this. She would freak. First, she would probably need legal counsel for attempting to murder Eugenia, if his mother didn't beat her to it, and then she would freak. He needed to talk to her, seriously, about this whole situation. He needed to convince her that he was in love with her, not just as friends but the "till death do us part" sort of love. He also needed everyone in his life to stop being so incredibly helpful where Devon was concerned.

He did what he always did when he was about to prepare closing arguments. He flicked on the power for his HO train and watched as the train began to move, whistling and churning. He had begun to marshal his thoughts by the time the caboose disappeared into the tunnel. Pat sat back to watch the soothing movement while formulating the most important strategy of his life.

The train puffed around its track, chugging up the mountain, then cheerfully puffing down the other side. The tiny people, eternally waiting at the station, stood motionless as it passed, once more on its way. A flag at the post office stood stiffly at attention as though a strong breeze held it aloft in the attic playroom.

Pat remembered when Devon had brought him through this house for the first time. He looked around the house and tried to see what Devon had fallen in love with, its history, integrity, challenge, whatever. It was simply too much of a stretch for his imagination and finally he had allowed that she *must* see something besides the leaking roof and sagging porch. He didn't see the magic but he trusted that Devon did. He knew that day it was a done deal as he watched her enthusiasm sparkle through each room.

Devon had taken one look at it and had known exactly what it would look like. He saw a cracked and ugly ceiling; she saw a timeless work of art. He looked at the obsolete plumbing and saw a nightmare; she saw a wonderful challenge. She loved the upstairs water closet next to the master bedroom. It was an original, with cherry wood paneling from floor to ceiling and built-in drawers for linens and necessities.

"This room would be a great nursery," she had told him.

"Excuse me?" he had asked, startled.

"You're one of those 'one and a half kids, a wife, and a big dog' kind of guys. You're going to need a nursery. This room would be perfect," she had told him, walking around, caressing the antique wood, scarred, but lovely and warm to touch. Like everything else in this house it had been built right.

Pat remembered arguing. "I was thinking it would make a great closet." He had added hopefully, "Maybe even a whirlpool."

Devon had shrugged. "Sure, until you need it for a nursery."

They had walked up the narrow stairs to the dusty, old attic and Devon had sparkled with plans for this, her favorite part of the house. The pitched roof met the scarred, hardwood flooring at a sharp and dusty angle as sunlight filtered through the cobwebs. This was the one area though that Pat had gotten excited about as he pictured exactly where he would build a model train set.

"This would be great for a kids' playroom," she decided. "I can see a wooden rocking horse in the corner and lots of toys and pillows and stuff for kids to play with."

"Your biological clock is ticking, isn't it?" he grumbled, thinking of electrical outlets and track designs.

"No. I'm just saying this is a wonderful play room," she had stubbornly argued.

"I was kind of thinking of putting my train set in here."

"That could go in the basement," she had reasoned. "You could finish the walls and put in a nice-sized model, even one of those L-shaped ones and your wife wouldn't have a fit about the mess."

"Maybe I'll marry someone who likes trains," he had told her.

"Sorry, women don't get into little trains like men do," she said, grinning. "Although, it is pretty cute the way a grown man can get so involved in something so silly."

"Trains are not silly and they're not cute. They are perfectly logical. You plan them, you build them, you enjoy them. That's what's so great about them," the attorney in him had argued.

Pat remembered her walking around, lost in imagining what the room would look like. He could see her building a picture in her mind, one he would burst the first weekend after he moved in, when he stubbornly began building his train set.

Always a good sport, Devon even helped him build his model railroad, adding a reproduction of a Victorian train depot with little trees and people. It took forever to glue the green stuff onto the popsicle sticks for the trees and even longer to make the plaster form for the mountains. Through it all Devon was there. They spent one whole Saturday up to their elbows in gooey plaster, dipping paper towels in the stuff and then laying it down over scrunched-up newspaper.

Devon was skeptical it could ever look like anything, but after it had dried and been painted, it was perfect. Pat let her design the village and even put a small lake on one side for her. She admitted when it was finished that it was fun building something that actually worked the way it was supposed to. Not like life at all. In her little world, no one dumped pollutants in her lake or released noxious fumes into the air. No one tore down her beautiful "painted lady" houses to make room for cement office buildings. It was paradise.

Paradise. Pat ran a hand through his hair. In a hectic, chaotic, wonderful way, that was what Devon brought into his life. She took the S-curves and derailments and made him laugh over them and made the smooth stretches even better. In time they compromised on the water closet, leaving it intact and sans Jacuzzi, but she remodeled his bath to include a state-of-the-art whirlpool bath. Then, he squelched her dreams for the attic. Pat sat staring at his train as a thought began forming. A grin started and spread from ear to ear as he grabbed the phone and called his brother.

"Can you come over here? I need some help moving something."

"It's a good thing you made the legs detachable," Dan grunted an hour later as they lifted the top of the table, track, mountains, and all.

"I just hope it fits through the door," Pat groaned as they inched the massive creation toward the tiny attic door.

"And three flights of stairs," Dan reminded him.

Pat rewarded him with a glare as they stood balancing the monstrosity at the narrow attic doorway. "Turn it to your right and we'll just angle it sideways through the door."

Moving in unison, they smoothly turned the table on its side and had a split second of satisfaction in knowing the mountains would just fit through the doorway.

Until they slid right off the table and the entire plaster world crashed to the floor, leaving them choking in dust with the remains of the town in a heap at their feet.

"Amazing," Pat said in quiet awe.

Dan shot him a startled look. They moved back in the room and placed the now-empty table on the floor. Pat cautiously advanced on the catastrophe heaped by the door and sat on his haunches. "Oh man, she's gonna kill me," he said, resting his forehead in his palm. "First that stupid magazine cover and now this."

"What does this have to do with the magazine cover?" Dan began.

"Everything. Just when I think I have it all figured out," he said, looking at the disaster, "nothing goes the way it's supposed to."

Dan came to squat next to him, handing him a soda as they looked at the disaster. They both knew Pat had enjoyed building the model as much as he enjoyed playing with it, so under normal circumstances he would look forward to an excuse to start over. But it seemed nothing was normal in his life anymore. Now, he had Devon. Or at least he had her until she saw what he'd done to their train set.

"She really loved this stupid thing," Pat muttered.

"Her perfect world. No pollution, no smog. A paradise," Dan cheerfully reiterated Devon's satisfaction. Pat glowered at him, frustrated with his feelings and not at all sure what he was doing anymore.

Dan took a deep drink of his soda, then casually asked, "Just what are we doing this for?"

"Devon always wanted to decorate the attic for a kids' play room and I thought . . ." he trailed off. "I don't know what I thought."

"You need a kids' play room?" Dan asked, arching an eyebrow.

"No," Pat told him glumly. "She does." He sighed in frustration. "This is stupid; I should have just left it the way it was. She's been avoiding me lately and then this stupid magazine came out and I thought this would be a great way to show her I am ready for a change. I want her to have the kids' playroom, but I guess making the change was a dumb idea."

"But nothing ever stays the way it was."

"Are you talking about the train or my relationship with Devon?" Pat asked.

"Both, but I think the train is going to be easier to build."

Pat snorted. "That's for sure. I must be nuts."

"No," Dan told him cheerfully. "I think you're just finally coming to your senses. You two are perfect for each other. If you don't drive each other crazy first."

"Thanks for the encouragement."

"All right. It's done." Dan apparently decided he would have to play the brisk brother this time, since Pat was completely unhinged by their beautiful redhead. "Let's finish moving it to the basement and we'll see what we can salvage from this."

Too discouraged to argue, Pat joined him. They spent the rest of the morning moving the debris to the basement and salvaging trees, track, and town buildings. Pat even started feeling a little more cheerful as they worked in the nearly finished basement. Devon was right. There really was a lot more room here. He could build a U-shaped layout with multiple levels and even different scale track if he planned it right.

As Pat enthused about the project, Dan glanced at his watch and stretched his shoulders. Then they froze, looking at each other in disbelief as they heard the door slam. Pat thought for one insane moment that he would be lucky and it might just be a burglar. The dog's joyous bark killed that hope as Dorky nearly knocked them down, bolting up the stairs to greet Devon.

Dan gave him a harassed look. "I told her you asked us to come over and help with some project. I thought it was a great excuse to get her over here. I didn't know you were going to destroy anything."

Pat raced for the stairs as Devon appeared at the top. "Hi, sweetheart," he gave her an overzealous hug, while Dan tried to shut the basement door behind them. "How was work? Did you raise lots of money this week? Is the remodeling done yet? Do you want something to drink?"

Pat eased her toward the kitchen as Devon gave him a bewildered look. She glanced to Dan for help while Pat knew he was prattling on. Dan was trying unsuccessfully to push a piece of evidence under the kitchen counter before she could see it.

"What have you two been up to?" she asked with narrowed eyes.

They shared an innocent, caught-in-the-cookie-jar

look. Then she stooped to the floor and help up a chunk of painted plaster. She gave Pat a questioning look. "Where did this come from?" Turning it over, she frowned, looking at the paint. "It almost looks like part of . . ." She looked at them in horror before bolting up the stairs.

"Devi, wait!" Pat called after her.

Wait? Not likely, Devon thought, racing up the attic stairs. He wouldn't have. He couldn't have. She bolted through the door. He had.

She stopped so quickly, Pat nearly ran her over. Looking around the empty attic, Devon swallowed back the lump in her throat. She would be rational. For once in her life, she would be rational. It was just a train. A stupid toy. And it wasn't even hers. She had no right to feel like bursting into tears because Pat had moved her little world. She had spent the morning crying already. Now, the enormous sugar high from the chocolate binge with Leslie was apparently wearing off as well. Maybe she should have stayed in bed today.

"Where is your train?" She marveled at the calm in her voice.

Pat tried to catch his breath and started explaining. "Umm, we put it in the basement and . . ."

He was fast reaching for her but she was faster. He missed catching her before she glided down the three flights of stairs and skidded to a stop with the heap of plaster at her feet. Pat panted to a halt behind her and started rambling about more room and better wiring and something that sounded like a playroom. For an excellent attorney he seemed to be floundering badly here.

That was just fine, she thought. He could talk all he wanted, the verdict was already in. He was an idiot. The curse hadn't just ruined his life, it had addled his brain as well. Devon clenched her fists looking at the total destruction of something that had been so special. It had been a symbol of her feelings for him when she put so much of her heart into his hobby. She thought he knew that train had been about her giving him what he wanted. It was about her compromising for him, which was something he was much better at. It had come to symbolize the give and take she loved about their relationship.

Apparently Pat had not caught on to its significance. Typical man, she thought, trying not to grind her teeth. He had gotten bored with his toy so he had heartlessly thrown it away. He probably didn't even care about the stupid magazine cover. She swallowed hard as she thought about that wretched fiasco. Fine. She could be just as cool. She calmly stalked past him and walked up the stairs. Fine, he could wallow in his plaster dust. She had a salad to murder. With any luck he would choke on an olive.

Pat hurried after her and then stopped as she serenely began unloading groceries in the kitchen. She was going to fix dinner. He shook his head. He had been worried she would be upset by the events of the day and she was calmly fixing dinner as though nothing had happened.

He gritted his teeth. He demolished his train and wasted an afternoon trying to please her and she didn't even care anyway. That was just dandy. He ran a frustrated hand through his gritty hair until she unloaded a can of anchovies onto the kitchen counter so hard it sounded like a bullet ricocheting in the house. Pat looked at her again, appraising, and saw the tension in her stance and the way she refused to look at him as she moved around the kitchen. Even Pandora whined and sank onto the floor, watching her with sad, brown eyes as Devon began washing romaine lettuce for a salad. He felt elated. She did care! She really cared about his train! He walked over and picked her up, swinging her around in a circle before kissing her soundly. He saw the absolute fury in her eyes before she masked it with a cool expression.

He grinned back. "I better go shower," he told her with another kiss.

Devon looked like she might throw the chicken kabobs at him before he cheerfully ran upstairs. While she continued to bang around in the kitchen, Pat whistled a merry tune, and started planning how he would make her little paradise the most perfect Garden of Eden an HO scale train set could hope to be.

Downstairs, Devon gave Dan a withering look. "Was this your idea?" she accused.

He leaned a hip against the counter and crossed his arms. "No. It was your idea."

"What?"

"Pat seems to think you never forgave him for putting the train in the attic. He just destroyed his favorite pastime so you could make a kids' playroom in his attic. Although, why you would want a nursery in Pat's attic is beyond me." He grinned and popped an olive in his mouth.

"He did that for me?" Devon's heart spun at the possibility.

Dan kissed her on the forehead and grabbed his keys. "Have fun." He turned at the door and gave her a thoughtful look. "Be gentle with him, okay?"

Pat whistled as he came downstairs. Even if Devon were still feeling murderous, it wouldn't last long. She might have a furious temper, but it never lasted more than a brief time, sort of like a seismic tremor. He entered the kitchen and saw the salad on the counter, the kabobs waiting to be grilled, but no Devon. He looked around, frowning. This annoying habit of disappearing whenever he entered the house was driving him crazy. Then he heard a soft "Woof!" from the nether regions upstairs.

She wasn't in the small bedroom that needed painting and she wasn't in any of the other rooms. Scrambling up the attic stairs, he breathed a sigh of relief. She was still here, sweeping up the carnage of the train disaster.

"You don't have to clean that up," he told her, waiting warily to see if he should duck.

"I don't mind. I had forgotten how big this room is," she said looking around.

Noting she was in a remarkably subdued mood, he looked around the attic. Funny, he had never noticed all the little touches she added over the years. The Union Pacific sign he and Dan liberated as kids hung in the center of one wall, surrounded by framed posters of trains. Even the light fixture was a model of an iron wheel; where she had found it, he had no idea. Swallowing a lump in his throat, he realized how much she had given to this sanctuary for him, and the heart of it now lay in a desecrated pile in his basement.

He nearly jumped when her fingers slipped into his. "It can all be moved," she said softly. "You actually have a better space in the basement for this. And we can add lots of track lighting to brighten it up. Maybe even put in a little refrigerator so you don't have to run upstairs every time you want something to drink."

"Thank you," he said softly. "For this. I never realized how nice you made it."

She shrugged. "It's what I do," she reminded him. "Could you do me a favor though?"

"Anything," he promised.

"Next time you feel like demolishing something in this house, could you warn me?"

He grinned at her, as she tried not to smile back.

"Either that, or make sure I've left the country. I don't think my heart could take another surprise."

"No problem. When I rip out the cherry wood in the

water closet, I'll call you first." He laughed out loud as her jaw dropped.

She narrowed her eyes suspiciously. "You wouldn't dare."

He picked up the dustpan and bent to clean the debris. Slanting a mischievous look at her, he said, "You should know better than to dare me, Devi."

Devon couldn't help smiling in return as she walked downstairs. She missed that easy give and take she enjoyed with Pat. As she set the table, she wondered briefly what it would be like to love a man and have this precious friendship as well. It would be a bit like having the proverbial cake and eating it, too, she imagined.

As Pat joined her she handed him the kabobs and watched him take them outside to the grill. In the recent mayhem of their relationship she had missed Pat. Now she vowed to enjoy this dinner. The prospect of a peaceful evening together was something she would never take for granted again. The music was playing, the food was cooking, and Devon looked at the perfection of it all. Then, she rubbed a hand over her heart and fiercely told herself it was enough.

Throughout dinner Devon found herself slowly relaxing. Pat seemed wonderfully unaware of the havoc he created with a simple look and they talked comfortably about work, family, and plans for the rest of the summer. He said with some relief that his assistant would be returning from Alaska next week and they both mentioned how much time Dan was spending with

Sunny lately. They talked about everything but the magazine cover.

As they cleared the table, they fell into an old routine. Devon rinsed dishes and loaded the dishwasher while Pat put away food and cleaned the dining room. It was all wonderfully normal until she started the dishwasher and turned around and ran into Pat's chest. He put his hands gently on her hips and kissed her ever so lightly. "Thank you," he said.

Devon was hoping her eyes weren't as crossed as they felt. "For what?"

"Dinner. You. I don't think I've ever told you how much I enjoy everything we do together."

Devon took a deep breath and stepped back. Arching an eyebrow in disbelief she countered, "Even stripping paint off the porch?"

He chuckled. "Okay, maybe not everything. Speaking of the porch, why don't we sit out there?" He had that gorgeous, determined look on his face again and Devon tried to think of an excuse to grab her keys and run. His eyes narrowed as he read her mind. "Unless you are afraid to."

She pursed her lips and squinted back. "Them's fighting words, Lawrence."

He picked up her Pendleton bag filled with sketches and carried it to the swing on his back porch. Devon picked up the glasses of fresh-brewed iced tea and followed. The back porch lay deep enough to house a table and chairs on one side while the other side bore a wrought iron swing Devon had found at a flea market.

Refinished in shiny white paint and layered with cushions, it was one of her favorite pieces in this home.

As Devon sat in the swing and put her glass on the side table, she thought of the hundreds of times she and Pat had sat here. She loved to rock here no matter what the weather. During a rain storm it felt like a cozy perch to smell the earth rejuvenating and in the heat of summer it offered shade and a cool breeze. Now in the warm evening air it seemed like a tranquil postcard in a hectic day. From here she could smell the English roses at the edge of the porch as well as lavender and rosemary from the side herb garden. The clematis climbing the corner post bloomed again, layered with extravagant purple blossoms. Birds chattered in the cherry tree in the neighbor's yard and Dorky ran to inspect every inch of the yard in case something had changed in the past hour.

Pat joined her with a file folder and notebook. He propped one ankle over his other knee and took a deep breath. "Your roses smell good," he told her.

"They're your roses," she said in return. "You had to dig the holes and mix the fertilizer."

The corner of his mouth lifted in humor. "Don't remind me. Although I do seem to get a lot of practice shoveling it at work these days."

"The parking meters?"

"Yep." He raised an arm and put it comfortably on the back of the swing, a move he had done dozens of times before. So why did her mouth go dry? She took a sip of her tea and tried to smell the roses but all she could smell was Pat's clean, masculine scent.

"Removing the parking meters was the trade-off for businesses saving the youth center and everyone agreed to it then, but now the budget department is howling. We discussed all of this before but since the youth center crisis calmed down they want to back out of losing those twenty meters."

"What's their angle?"

"They claim it will leave an unsightly imbalance to the design of those blocks." He chuckled. "I never realized how attractive parking meters could be to some people."

Devon smiled and then caught her breath as he began to gently massage her neck. She breathed deep and told herself to relax. "Doug in street design called and asked for advice. I sent over some streetscape plans with lanterns and hanging planters but they cost money so I imagine the budget folks will change their tune."

"I can't wait to see what they come up with next." Pat sipped his drink and continued to rub her neck, the sensuous warmth stealing through her. They fell into an easy rhythm, rocking and listening to the night sounds. Dorky gave up her explorations and collapsed at their feet. Her head used Devon's foot for a pillow. She knew the other foot would soon rub her ears. Devon felt her silky fur and sighed. She really loved it here. She loved the smells and sounds and feel of everything about this place.

That appreciation for her surroundings always made her wonder what the original inhabitants were like. Did they sit on this porch after a long day working the rich fields that surrounded the house a hundred years ago? Did the husband rub his wife's neck this way after the children were put in their beds and the livestock fed for the night? She hoped so.

The water fountain at the other corner of the house added a soothing melody while Devon thought about the Rosemary mansion. The people who lived in it led more affluent lives than the farmers who lived here. Still, there were so many loving details the owner had built into the house for his wife. Some of those touches added to the architectural value of the museum, but many made it tough to meet modern visitors needs.

The first owner made sure his wife had a beautiful, sunny room for her sewing, taking space from the hall and other bedrooms to give her a haven for her delicate handiwork. Coordinating the narrow hallways upstairs with fire codes and furniture movers now made it an architectural headache. She started sketching an idea she came across in a design magazine earlier that day. Dorky started to softly snore and twitch in her sleep, probably dreaming about chasing the acrobatic squirrels that raided Pat's birdfeeders.

They each worked in companionable silence for a while. Finally Pat yawned and put the paperwork aside.

"Tired?" she asked as he stretched. She loved the elegant way his arms flexed.

"Yes. I didn't realize how late it is," he responded.

"Well, it's pretty hard work destroying your favorite pastime."

He gave her a concerned look. "I did it for you," he blurted out.

His beautiful eyes filled with worry and she squeezed his hand. "I know. It's all right. Pat . . . about the magazine."

"I heard Eugenia is off your mom's Christmas list," he said in a dry tone.

"I heard your mom wanted to bury her at the cabin but your dad talked her out of it," she responded.

"This curse thing," he said, massaging her palm with his thumb. "I don't want it to come between us. I don't want it to interfere with our lives."

"I wonder if it has. Maybe in time things would have changed anyway."

"I don't want some things to change though," Pat told her. "I love having you in my life, my home, my family. I don't ever want that to change."

Devon tried to think of a response when the front gate creaked. She looked up to see two teenage girls walking shyly up to the porch.

"Hi, are you the McKenzie Man?" one of them asked.

Pat really needed to stop grinding his teeth like that, Devon thought. It wasn't good for him, even though she could understand it. These girls couldn't be over sixteen.

"I'm Pat Lawrence," he replied carefully.

"Could we take your picture? I mean with us. We just live down the street and our friends didn't believe that we knew you."

Devon was pretty sure they didn't know him but she saw how polite and nervous they were. "Why don't I take your pictures with him?"

Pat gave her a look of disbelief. She lined the girls up on either side and told them to smile. She clicked the picture and remembered another girl who had worn his sweatshirt for an entire year. She handed the camera back to the girls and they thanked Pat and then ran out of the yard giggling.

"They are starting younger," he said in a gloomy tone.

"Maybe we're just getting older," she said sitting down. He joined her, picking up her hand and continuing the tender massage. They watched the faint streaks of sunset paint the sky.

"Devon," he said in a serious tone, "can we talk?"

She bit her lip and wondered if he could feel her heart hammering in her chest. "It depends," she told him. She tried to give him a bright smile. "If it's serious, I may need more brownies."

"I've been thinking about the curse and how it seems to affect people," he said.

You mean like giving your best friend the hots for you? she thought. As much as she would like to blame the curse though, she had fought these feelings for Pat before. Each time she told herself she would never do anything to endanger their precious friendship. Now she wondered if that's what she really wanted. She had loved Pat her whole life and now she wanted it to be so much more than a friendship. The gift of that friendship was so precious that the thought of risking it was terrifying.

He watched her in the fading light. "What are you thinking?"

"That I wish things could stay the same," she said.

He swallowed hard. "Oh." He shifted and mulled that for a moment. "What are you feeling?"

"Fear."

"Fear," he repeated, sounding surprised. "You're the most fearless person I know."

"I'm afraid of losing something really precious."

He sighed and kissed the top of her head. "You won't. No matter what," he promised. "You are very precious to me," he told her.

"You are to me, too," she said, looking into the shadows around his eyes. "I don't want to lose you," she whispered.

Pat rested his forehead against hers. "You're stuck with me, sweetheart."

Devon put her head on his chest and wrapped her arms around him. She could hear his heart beating, solid and steady. "Good."

Chapter Twelve

Pat tied his shoelaces and stretched his calves. He just had time for a long run before he showered for work. He tucked his spare key into the Velcro pocket on his running shoe and thought how well things seemed to be going with Devon. The train debacle started out as badly as a surprise witness for the opposition, but in the end it worked beautifully. Devon was speaking to him again and he was ready for stage two as soon as he figured out what that would be. The phone rang and he debated not answering, but saw Devon's number on the caller ID.

"Morning, sweetheart," he said, smiling at the thought of her sipping coffee in her favorite overstuffed chair.

"Pat, could you pl-please come over?" Devon's tearful voice on the phone nearly knocked the wind from Pat's lungs.

"Honey, I'm on my way." He disconnected the phone and raced for the door then stopped. If he bolted over the back fence and took a shortcut through a couple of neighbors' yards he would be there in a minute. He nearly did, too, thinking he could do it in superhuman time from the adrenaline. No, he might need a car for this emergency. *Dear God,* he prayed, *don't let her be hurt.* What if something happened to her? As his car screeched to a stop in front of her house, he couldn't imagine his life without Devon.

Devon appeared at the door, tears streaming down her face. Thankfully, she could walk. Whatever upset her, it didn't matter. He would take care of it.

"Honey, I'm here," he gathered her quivering body in his arms and tried to comfort her with every ounce of his being. "What happened?"

"It's Charlie," she cried.

"Charlie?" Stunned, Pat tried to think what her wretched cat could have done to upset her so. He had seen Devon weather some tough times, and he'd never seen her fall apart like this. "What did that stupid animal do now?"

"He's not stupid," she wailed. "He's dead."

"Oh," was all he could think of saying as he scooped her up in his arms and walked into the living room. Sitting on the couch, he cradled her helplessly while she cried.

Well, this is just dandy, he thought. He still didn't have a brilliant strategy for stage two but he was pretty sure it wouldn't have included this. She sniffled softly into his chest and he sighed. Stage two could wait. The last thing his tender-hearted lady needed now was to feel pressured about their relationship. Stupid cat.

Pat kissed the top of her head. "I'm so sorry, sweetheart." He soothed and rocked her, stroking her hair and trying madly to think of something to make her feel better. The sound of her sobs tore through his chest, making him feel helpless and frustrated. She hadn't cried this hard when Dan broke her arm. Or when that idiot Mike Thompson had broken her heart in high school. Wretched animal. He'd wring its neck, he thought, then grimaced. Unfortunately, he wouldn't get the pleasure since the beast had obviously run out of lives.

"Honey, what happened?" He was almost afraid to ask, considering Charlie's eight other lives had been rather kamikaze.

"I don't know. He didn't wake me up this morning and I found him in his kitty bed," she gulped. "I thought he was asleep, but he wouldn't wake up," she explained with a little sniffle.

"Honey, he was very old, he probably just died from old age."

"But he was so healthy. He even ate two slices of pizza last night." She looked at him with huge, tragic eyes. "Maybe there was something wrong with it."

"Did you eat it?"

"Yes."

"And you feel okay?"

"Yes, but he was just a helpless kitty!" she wailed. "I should have taken better care of him. The vet said I should watch his diet. I shouldn't have given him pizza!"

"Devi, he was old, the oldest cat I've ever heard of. I really don't think he was complaining about the way you spoiled him. He was a happy, healthy cat and it was just his time to go to kitty heaven." Pat unconsciously slipped into the logic he had used when she was a child.

A hysterical little giggle bubbled from her lips. "Do you really think that's where he went?"

No, Pat thought. *Not a chance.* "Of course, sweet-heart. He was a wonderful cat." *For you,* he silently added.

Devon gulped as fresh tears fell. "I miss him so much," she cried.

"Honey, it's okay. We'll find you a new kitty, I promise."

"You can't just replace him like that, it's not the same." She stubbornly shook her head.

Pat gritted his teeth and reminded himself that this was Devon he was trying to reason with. He should just shut up and wait until she was in a reasoning mood. All he could do, had ever been able to do at this point, was offer comfort.

Devon felt his arms tighten about her as she settled against his chest. She tried to tell herself that Pat couldn't understand how she felt. He had never liked Charlie. *So why had she called him?* It had been instinctive, of course. She hadn't even considered calling anyone else. Resting in his arms, she could feel that old sense of calm enveloping her, familiar and so very dear.

Pat was always the one she turned to when she was hurting, the first person she called with good news, and the one whose company she sought at any time. What was this bond between them that made every other relationship pale? It was more than just sharing a lifetime of history together. She shared that with Dan and while she loved Dan dearly, it was nothing compared to the feelings that welled in her heart for Pat. She tilted her face to him, catching a tender look that made her heart ache.

"Feeling better?" he asked softly. He ran his thumb over her cheek, gently wiping away the tears. "I'm sorry, honey. I know how much you loved Charlie. He was a great cat for you."

Fresh tears filled her eyes. "Thank you. I know you hated him."

Pat shook his head. "I didn't hate him. I just don't like animals that are smarter than I am," he said with a rueful smile.

"That explains Dorky," she tried to tease back, but hiccupped shakily instead.

Pat lay his hand on her cheek. He bent his head, kissing her ever-so-softly on the forehead, then her eyes and cheeks. Devon waited for him to reach her lips, but instead he rested his forehead against hers. After a moment he shifted her out of his arms.

"Do you want me to take care of him?"

Devon was confused for a moment, then felt a fresh wave of grief. She had to make some decisions. "I want to bury him."

"Where? I don't think Mrs. Baxter would appreciate us digging up her geraniums, even if that was his favorite spot."

Devon looked to see if Pat was teasing her but he had that gentle, big-brother look on his face. She bit her lip, knowing he would think she was crazy.

"We could call one of those pet cemeteries. Maybe plan a little memorial for him," she suggested.

Pat opened his mouth to argue, then closed it. He nodded. "I'll make a few calls. Wait here." He covered her with a soft quilt, tucking her in. After fixing her a cup of hot, herbal tea, he promised, "I'll be right back."

Pat closed the office door and took a deep breath. He was insane. The logical part of his brain said those animal cemeteries were ridiculous scams. But then he thought of the hurt in Devon's eyes and picked up the phone book. He'd gladly pay the piper if it made her feel better.

After two phone calls Pat found one that sounded somewhat legitimate. He made the arrangements, then walked to the cat's bed in the sunny window seat. He almost expected the creature to look at him with that smug "Gotcha" look it had been giving him for two decades. Unfortunately, it didn't.

Following the cemetery's instructions, Pat gingerly moved the lifeless little body around the house, out of Devon's view, and onto the porch. Oddly, he felt a wave of grief as well. They may have been adversaries but they had both loved the same woman. He stroked the soft fur, thinking of the wretched little thing it had been when he rescued it and the pampered fat cat it had become, and ultimately how much love it had given Devon. As many times as he had threatened the little bugger, he was glad it lived such a spoiled and lengthy life.

Then, he felt like an idiot as he returned to the house, looking for the beast's favorite toy. After looking in Devon's bedroom, the laundry, and an old pair of his shoes by the porch, he spotted it under a chair.

Devon sipped her tea and watched, bemused, as Pat searched the house. She was afraid to ask what he was up to, but trusted him just the same. He looked like a man on a mission, that determined look making a fine furrow between his eyebrows. Finally he knelt down and retrieved Charlie's battered little catnip mouse. Standing up, he gave her an embarrassed look.

"They said they usually bury them with a favorite toy."

"I love you," she said softly. Heaven help her. She really did.

Pat froze, giving her a look of complete astonishment. He looked like she had just hit him alongside the head instead of making the most terrifying admission of her life. She waited for his response, then watched, as he turned with a blank look on his face and carried the mouse to the porch.

He came in, washed his hands, and poured himself a cup of coffee. With some concern, she noted his hands shook holding the cup. She couldn't discern what was going on in that brilliant mind of his, but he downed the coffee in a rush, then poured more. When he faced her, he had his features carefully masked.

Well, she decided, if she were going to jump off an emotional cliff, who better to do it with than the man who had always been there to catch her? She waited patiently as he sat next to her and cradled her in his arms again. Still, no response. The man was impossible. A car drove up to the house and they heard footsteps. The porch squeaked for a moment, then the footsteps retreated, taking the cat away.

Pat cleared his throat. "They can do the memorial tomorrow after work if you'd like."

Devon nodded. "That would be fine."

He cleared his throat. "Do you want me to stay with you? Take the day off?" he asked.

"No, I have some floor plan revisions at work I should finish. It'd be better if I keep busy. Thank you, though." Devon stood up, determined to get moving.

Pat rose, taking the tea from her and obviously searching for something to say.

"Thank you," she told him. "I don't know what I'd do without you."

"That's what friends are for," he told her softly.

Devon flinched, then hurried upstairs before he could see her cry anymore. Friends. That was pretty obvious, she told herself. She didn't need a doctorate to figure out what Pat wanted from her. Friendship, nothing more.

As she lay out clothes for work, she took a deep breath. It had been a little game she played with Charlie. She would lay out clothes and when she came out of the shower, he would be sitting on them. No matter what she did, he would find a way to get his furry little hide on her outfit. A wave of loneliness swept over her as she reached for the lint brush and then put it down. No need for it today.

She trudged downstairs, eager to get out of the house and its memories. Instead, Pat met her with a breakfast of her favorite muffins and orange juice. He must have run to the store while she showered. Then he hovered over her through the meal, chatting about nonsense and trying to keep her mind occupied.

Devon watched him trying to entertain her and wondered if she could survive this. Not losing Charlie; that still didn't feel real yet. She wasn't sure she could survive Pat's friendship. She had thought it the most important thing, the part of their relationship to protect at all costs. She was wrong. She wanted more and being around him now simply made it worse.

"I better be going," she told him softly. "I really appreciate everything, Pat." She kissed him on the cheek softly before fleeing the house.

Obviously Dan was wrong about his brother's feelings. That was a real shock, she told herself sarcastically. When was the last time Dan was right about anything? Her heart was too battered to worry about it, though, as she drove to work alone.

Pat watched her drive away as he tried to form a

coherent thought. It was all he had been trying to do since she looked at him with the world shining in her eyes and said, "I love you."

So much for stage two. He looked thoughtfully at Mrs. Baxter's geraniums and thought perhaps the fur-ball hadn't really been so bad after all.

Devon was about to leave for the memorial service when a shadow crossed her desk. Looking up, she saw Pat standing there. "You came," she said in surprise.

He shrugged. "It seemed fitting. We started out together," he told her. "Charlie and I."

He looked uncomfortable and probably wished he could be going anywhere but to a memorial for a cat. A cat that had tormented him since childhood, she reminded herself. Still, he was here for her and she should be grateful. She had been feeling unbearably lonely without her furry roommate in spite of the best efforts of her friends and family.

Leslie and Morgan kept her busy last night, not because of anything truly critical at work, but because they didn't want her going home to an empty house. Then her father arrived and bustled her home where her mother's pot roast and her old room waited for her. She felt a bit guilty for feeling so lonely without Charlie when she was so very lucky to have so many people care for her. Now this wonderful man stood at her desk ready to sit through a memorial for a cat that once chewed through and spit up his favorite fishing lure.

Raising on tiptoe, she kissed his cheek. "Thank you," she said softly.

He nodded, giving her a sweet look that nearly made her cry again. Pat glanced at the pretty geranium pot in her hands.

"Mrs. Baxter gave it to me. To plant with . . . you know," she finished softly. Pat took her hand in his and walked to his car. As they drove, a stilted silence filled the car. She toyed with the geraniums and looked out the window. The cemetery was on the outskirts of town, fifteen minutes from her office. They pulled up to the address, a sign in front proclaiming HEAVENLY HAVEN. Under it another sign announced EVERLASTING TAXIDERMY.

They walked to the lovely old house—early 1920s, Devon guessed as she surveyed the sloped roof and multipaned windows. A portly woman opened the door, beaming at them from a sweetly rounded face.

"Hello, dear. I'm Willow Jorgenson. Come in. We have everything ready in back." Willow ushered them in. "Would you like some tea first?"

Devon shook her head and clutched Pat's hand, sensing his attorney instincts working overtime. Now was not the time for him to be logical and protective. If he said a word, she'd make him sit in the car, she thought grimly.

Willow led them through the kitchen and into a large backyard. A connecting gate led them to the next lot, fenced, landscaped, and dotted with tiny markers. They stopped at a newly dug space and waited. A little cedar box was lying on the ground, a lace cloth with "Charlie" embroidered in the corner adorned its top.

Devon looked about the pretty yard. A huge Norway maple shaded the little graveyard with sweet-smelling roses around the perimeter. Rows of flowers broke up the yard into different areas. A glance behind her showed a fairly good-sized plot with a marker for "Brutus."

Willow smiled for her. "This is one of my favorite spots. I'm glad we're putting such a special animal here.

She could feel Pat stiffen. At least he didn't snort in derision. "He was very special," Devon said softly. "But, I guess they all are."

"Yes, but most aren't as old as this one. I don't know that we've ever seen a kitty so old or so well cared for. He even had a little smile on his face," Willow told her cheerfully.

Pat made a soft strangling sound and Devon shot him a warning look.

"So nice to see animals die of old age so peacefully," Willow continued breezily. Then a flustered look crossed her rather vacant expression. "I don't mean it's nice to see them go. Of course we wish they would live forever. But then, of course, we wouldn't have a business," she finished.

Devon thought she felt Pat's shoulders shaking but she couldn't kick him in the shins with the sweet, albeit ditzy Willow standing there. She stole a glance at him, catching the pained look on his face that he promptly masked to give her an encouraging look. She made a mental note to buy him an extra birthday present this year, just for behaving like he hadn't wanted to hasten Charlie's demise himself a few times over the years.

An older man joined them, introducing himself as Mr. Jorgenson. He gave Devon a sympathetic look and asked if the spot was all right.

"It's perfect. Thank you," she told him, instantly liking his kind features and the gentle look he gave his wife.

"Willow was quite taken by your kitty," he confided to Devon. "She thought he would be beautiful mounted on a favorite pillow, but your young man was adamant you wanted a burial."

Devon could hear Pat's teeth grinding again. Somehow, she imagined Charlie sitting over them, enjoying this scene immensely. With a much lighter heart, she shook her head, "This is fine. Really."

Mr. Jorgenson read a little poem about cats roaming fields of flowers for eternity. Devon couldn't help but sniff as he placed the little box in the ground. At least Charlie would have liked this place.

"We'll leave you some time alone," Willow told them, patting Devon's hand before she and Mr. Jorgenson retreated from the garden.

Devon looked around as a breeze blew through the trees, rustling the leaves softly. A bird sang from somewhere in the massive foliage, oblivious of its former predators buried below. A faint scent of honeysuckle wafted around them, lightly mixed with Victorian roses.

"Charlie would have liked this place," she whispered.

"Lots of flowers to dig up," Pat whispered back.

Sacrilegious or not, Devon giggled. Pat took the geraniums and placed them next to the little grave. Then he took her hand and led her through the dainty stone walkway.

Devon sighed. "Did you see the marker for Priscilla?"

"Was that the one with the marble poodle?"

She couldn't help but giggle. "Oh Pat, I know it was crazy, but I feel better."

Pat squeezed her fingers. "Then it was worth it."

"How much did this cost me?"

"Don't worry about it," he said, pushing open the gate and leading her toward his car.

"Pat, you don't have to pay for it."

"I already did. Don't worry about it."

"You hated Charlie," she reminded him.

"I didn't hate Charlie." He didn't sound too convincing.

"Liar."

"I never lie," he told her.

"I know," she said, kissing him on the cheek. He wrapped his arms around her in a comforting hug. "I love you," she said unconsciously.

He stiffened for an instant then kissed the top of her head. Devon sighed. Taking a deep breath, she stepped back. She tried to tell herself it was better to have his precious friendship than nothing at all. Maybe if she told herself that enough times she would believe it.

As Devon slid into his car, she tried not to think of

the empty house she would be going home to. Yet in a crazy way, she did feel better after the little ceremony they had just witnessed. It must be part of that human obsession with closure, she thought. As much as Pat probably hated every second of it, he had stayed with her, holding her hand, gently massaging her fingers, lending his strength to her.

"Do you want to go home or do you want to do something?" he asked her.

She thought for a moment. "I don't think I want to go home."

"How about a movie?

"That would be fun," she said, trying to convince herself.

They found a movie playing at the mall, a romantic comedy that Devon could hardly pay attention to as Pat held her hand in his own throughout the show. The comfort of his arm overlapping hers helped her relax as she tried to concentrate on the movie. In her numbed state of loss, she only caught half the movie's punchlines.

Emotionally exhausted, she leaned her head against Pat's shoulder. In the midst of popcorn and people she could smell his scent, clean and masculine. She felt safe and cared for as he stayed with her. The only part of the movie she couldn't ignore was the love scene. It was a good thing the theater was dark because she blushed to her roots. Pat squeezed her fingers, rubbing his thumb over her palm gently as her imagination began to take on wild images.

With some relief, Devon sat up as the movie ended.

"What did you think?" Pat asked.

"I wasn't thinking," she admitted. "I guess I feel kind of numb."

Pat put his arm around her waist and walked her to the car. His stomach growled, causing Devon to smile. "I take it popcorn wasn't enough dinner."

"Hardly." He grinned back. "What do you feel like? We could get Chinese and eat at my house."

Devon shook her head. Always the planner, Pat was obviously thinking of ways to keep her from going home to an empty house.

"How about Delaney's Grill?" she asked, knowing it was his favorite. "My treat because you've been such a good sport."

"We could get something else. It's your choice, Dev. Pick something you like."

"I feel like a really greasy mushroom burger," she told him.

"A woman after my own heart," he approved.

I wish, she thought as they drove to the diner.

The hostess seated them at a booth in the fifties-style diner and Pat ordered a chocolate milk shake for Devon.

"You know how to spoil a girl," she told him appreciatively as she sipped the thick concoction.

"I hope so," he told her. "You deserve to be spoiled."

The waitress came to the table and stood shyly looking at Pat. Devon recognized the symptoms and waited. The girl pulled out a copy of *McKenzie Magazine,* the one with Pat's smiling face on the cover.

"Could you sign this?" she asked. Pat was decidedly pink about the ears as he graciously signed the picture.

"Thank you," the girl told him. "We've got all of them. The McKenzie Men, I mean. The owner wants to frame them and start a wall for them."

"An honor wall for Eugene's finest men," Devon said approvingly.

"No. He said it would be a memorial to the poor souls." The girl blushed scarlet and looked at Devon. "I mean a memorial to, umm . . ."

Devon was trying to keep a straight face. "The town's luckiest men?" she offered helpfully.

"Sure," the girl said with some relief. "That's it." She fled to the kitchen with the magazine clutched in her hands.

Devon looked at Pat and tried not to laugh at the look of consternation on his face. "Oh, Pat. I am sorry I got you into this."

He gave her a thoughtful look. "I'm not. Maybe the curse isn't such a bad thing after all."

Devon nearly choked on her shake. "How can you say that? After all you've been through?"

"Sometimes a crisis can be an eye-opening opportunity." He stirred his soda with the straw. "It's been a chance to see things in my life that I've always taken for granted." He captured her with an intense look. "Things I will never take for granted again."

The waitress appeared with their burgers and Devon gratefully started eating. She agreed with what he was saying. It had taken the past two miserable days for her to realize how deeply she loved him. She wondered what things he had realized. How important their friendship was, she thought. He made it clear that was what he wanted from her. Perhaps, in his own male fashion, he was just realizing what a special bond they shared. Having swallowed enough hurt in the past forty-eight hours, she refused to hope he had realized anything more significant than that.

"That really hit the spot," he told her, finishing the last of his fries. "Thank you."

She shook her head. "Thank you. I seem to be saying that a lot lately, but I mean it."

He held her hand as they left the diner. As he unlocked his car, Devon heard a metal banging sound, then a crash. She looked at Pat while he scowled, listening. Then they both heard it. A tiny mewing sound.

Devon started towards the darkened side of the diner. Pat grabbed her arm. "Stay here," he told her firmly.

Devon quietly tiptoed after him as he approached the toppled garbage can. He reached down for something, then she heard a muffled curse. She jumped a foot when a shadow flew past, skittering under the car.

Pat said something rude under his breath.

"Was that a kitten?" she asked.

Pat nodded, then sighed as he looked at her face. "I don't suppose you'd let me back my car up and let it take its chances?" he asked.

Devon punched him in the arm. "Stop kidding around. We have to get it out of there."

Pat retrieved a flashlight from his glove box. Handing

her his suit jacket, he lay on his stomach and peered under the car. Muttering something about a dry cleaning bill, he reached under the car, then swore as a furious kitten's cry broke the air. Pat stood up, holding the hissing and spitting furball. Then he let it go, yelping in pain.

"The little bugger bit me," he said, shaking his hand.

The kitten crashed into Devon's legs, its feet scraping madly on the pavement, trying to get purchase to flee. She scooped up the shaking little body and cuddled him in Pat's jacket, cooing and trying to calm him.

Pat shook his head, as the kitten finally settled down, burrowing its head under Devon's arm and waiting its fate. "I wonder if the humane society is open this late?" he asked hopefully.

"Pat! We can't take it to the humane society," she told him. "We need to take it home and see if it's hurt."

"Of course we do," Pat said, getting in the car and muttering something under his breath.

"What did you say?" she asked him.

"Nothing."

"I thought you said something about nine lives."

He shrugged. "I must have miscounted."

She wondered what he meant as she stroked the kitten. She made Pat stop at the grocery store and buy three different kinds of kitten food. He came out carrying a litter box and other necessities. Devon started to tell him she had those at home already but decided it could wait.

"How is your hand?"

"Fine. Thanks for asking," he said in an amused tone.

"Did it break the skin?"

"No. Not that it didn't try," he told her with a quick frown for the little ball of fur curled in her arms.

Devon sighed. She supposed he had been an exceptionally good sport through the past two days and it wasn't his fault he had developed an aversion to stray cats that bit him. She looked at the kitten and thought how odd that it had nearly the same markings as Charlie. She thought about her beloved cat and smiled. Maybe he did make it to kitty heaven after all and this was his way of helping her through the grief. She lay her cheek against the kitten as it clutched its paws into her neck. The kitten nuzzled back.

"I thought we were going to my house," she said in surprise, looking up at his driveway.

"I thought we could come here first. You said you didn't want another cat so soon."

"And you do?" she asked in disbelief. Pat shrugged as he reached for the kitten, then grimaced when it made a tiny, but distinct growling sound. "I'll bring the food in," he told her.

Inside, Pat found a bowl for the kitten and Devon worried over it while it stuffed its little belly with food. "Don't let it eat too much, or it might get sick." Pat offered helpfully, looking at the little creature as though it might do something disgusting on his polished hardwood floor at any moment.

Dorky sat in the doorway of the kitchen watching the furball with a look of wary animosity on her face. Finally deciding she wasn't going to be the center of attention, she stalked to her favorite spot and lay down to pout. Devon gave her a dog biscuit and rubbed her head.

"You're still top dog here," Devon told her.

Devon sat down as the kitten began to make his jaunty way around the house. His adventure took him near Dorky who lay perfectly still, a look of doggie cunning on her face.

Pat sat on the edge of the couch, next to Devon and waited warily for the coming confrontation. He stole a glance at Devon, wondering if he should retrieve the cat before it became dog food. Devon shook her head and continued watching the two.

As the kitten wandered toward the still dog, Pandora never blinked an eye. Pat watched, tensely waiting, as the kitten cautiously sniffed the dog, then approached the dog biscuit laying at the retriever's nose. Pat jumped as a low growl emanated from the dog's throat.

The kitten backed away quickly and arched its back. It looked perfectly ridiculous with its tiny tail in a frizzy puff. The game continued as the kitten explored other parts of the room, always returning to Pandora's biscuit, always warned with a low growl that it had gone too far.

Finally, the kitten appeared to lose interest as it entertained itself with a bit of paper from under a chair. Pat sighed in relief. "Well, I guess that's settled."

He left to pour two glasses of iced tea and congratulate himself on how well the transition was going. He walked back in the room just as the kitten nonchalantly sauntered past Pandora's nose, then snatched the biscuit. Before the cat could escape, the dog grasped the tiny furball in its mouth and flung it, biscuit and all across the room.

All Pat saw was a spinning, spitting ball of fur cartwheel across his living room. He looked at Devon, stunned, waiting for Pandora's demise, but Devon laughed at the spectacle. The dog calmly walked over, picked up her biscuit and returned to her original place. The sodden kitten proved it had no more brains than his dog when it marched smartly across the room and swiped the dog across her nose with a tiny paw. Pandora whimpered at the sting and rubbed her nose. Pat stood there, shocked, waiting for the cat to use up another one of its lives.

The two animals looked at each other in wary appraisal, then the kitten stalked around the retriever and arched its back lovingly against the dog's neck. The dog returned the good-natured rub with a gentle nudge of her nose and a kiss down the kitten's already doggy-wet coat. The cat continued its game with the paper and the dog began calmly eating its biscuit.

Devon grinned. *"Now* it's settled."

They watched the two play until the kitten became tired. Instead of using the box Pat had made with a soft pillow for a bed, it climbed on top of the dog's back and fell asleep, its little purr rattling through the room.

Devon yawned and looked at her watch. It was after midnight. Time to go home, to her empty house. She looked at Pat and he seemed to read her mind.

"Why don't you stay here tonight? Your car is still downtown and I can drive you in the morning."

At the moment, Devon had to admit her own house had little appeal.

Pat added. "The kitten seems comfortable here. It'd be a shame to move him. You could stay in the blue bedroom."

Devon bit her lip thoughtfully as she watched the sleeping kitten. The turmoil of the past few days was catching up to her as her mind felt incapable of making a rational decision. She slipped her hand in his and laid her head on his shoulder.

"The blue room will be fine," she told him.

He kissed the top of her head and said, "Why don't you take a hot bath? It might help you sleep. There are clean sweats and T-shirts in the bottom drawer of the wardrobe. I'll sit up with the furball for awhile."

She started to leave the room, then stood looking at him, wanting to say something more and yet not sure what. He looked at her, a dozen different emotions crossing his face. Afraid to say or do something she might regret, she simply walked upstairs.

The next morning she stopped in the doorway to the living room. She watched, amused, as Pat lay on the couch, covered by an afghan her mother had made for him. The kitten lay stretched out on his chest. "We're going to do this right this time," he said to the kitten, oblivious to Devon's presence. She bit back a smile. He sounded like a lawyer making closing arguments.

"I don't mind the hair on my clothes and I can live with your toys in my shoes, but I swear, there had better not be any more snakes. Understood?" The kitten purred and nuzzled his chin. "That's better. And if you promise to leave my fishing tackle alone, I'll even stick up for you when it's time to get fixed. Okay?"

The kitten stretched in his arms, kicked its tiny paws into the air and promptly fell asleep. Devon patted Dorky's head as she padded over in greeting. "Looks like you have a roommate," she told the dog. Dorky sneezed in response and stalked to her favorite spot, laying her head on her paws and giving Pat a put-upon look.

Pat blushed when he saw Devon standing there and realized she'd probably heard him talking to the furball. She wore a soft expression of adoration that he had seen a thousand times before. She slowly walked over to him, tucked the afghan around him and smiled.

Cupping his face in her hands, she told him, "You are the most wonderful man I know." Then she kissed him softly on the mouth and went into the kitchen to fix breakfast.

Pat stared after her, completely bewildered. He looked at the kitten sleeping in his arms, its white paws crossed over its scrawny chest. "I don't understand women. Do you?"

The kitten opened one eye, belched, and promptly fell asleep again.

"I didn't think so," he muttered.

Chapter Thirteen

Devon returned to her office after visiting the Rosemary mansion feeling more lighthearted than she had in days. The initial funding had come through and she spent the morning detailing the first phase of renovation to the workers. This was the most difficult part, shoring up the structural integrity of the house. After that the rest was window dressing, expensive and beautiful, but still window dressing.

She picked up her messages and the smile faded from her face. Two more messages from Pat. He had called her every day since Charlie's memorial, but she hadn't spoken with him since he dropped her off at work the next morning. He had driven away, still wearing that bemused look from when she kissed him. She knew she couldn't keep avoiding him forever. Not that she wasn't thinking about him day and night. In fact,

173

she was starting to feel a bit punchy from the emotions that swirled within her every time she thought of him.

She just wasn't ready to deal with him face to face yet. She could start to understand why they sequestered juries. No distractions, no helpful friends or relatives, no magazine publishers or waitresses. Just time to review the facts and come up with a decision.

Unfortunately, the kitten had taken up residence at Pat's house and hers was still uncompromisingly empty. Retrieving the kitten would mean facing Pat and she couldn't do that, not without fear that she would blurt out the kaleidoscope of emotions she felt toward him. She had never been one to mince words, but then she had never trodden such dangerous waters with the most important relationship in her life.

So, this week, she watched action movies with Dan until late, and dug with Leslie in the dirt until the dark and her aching back made them stop. She baked brownies and ate too many of them with her mother and played a game of chess with her dad that he pretended to lose. And every one of them managed to tell her what a wonderful guy Pat was.

She was starting to feel a bit like an ostrich with her head stuck in the sand. Now, her own impulsive instincts were beginning to win out. The feeling of being suspended over a pit of crocodiles was driving her mad. It took everything she had to not pick up the phone and demand to have this out.

First, she needed to get away and spend some time thinking. She needed some healing place where she could think clearly. One place came to mind. The cabin. Looking at her watch, she thought of a plan. She could pack a bag on her lunch hour and leave straight from work. It seemed like a very good plan.

Hours later, Devon looked at her watch and groaned. Two hours late. She'd stayed at work to finish a proposal that the board decided it needed immediately and now she was driving to the cabin in the dark. It was a very good thing she could make the drive with her eyes closed. Just driving along the winding road began to calm her nerves. She began to breathe more deeply, feel more relaxed.

It would be a chance to marshal her thoughts and decide how to deal with Pat, without worrying about seeing him around every corner. Then she pulled into the cabin and couldn't believe her luck. She sat there staring at Pat's SUV in disbelief. It never occurred to her that he might come here too. For one horrible moment she wondered if he had brought someone with him, but, then the door opened and Pat walked out alone. Seeing him was the last straw. Devon felt like doing what she had done all her life—run to his arms, put her head on his shoulder and cry, but this time she couldn't.

Pat opened her car door. "Hi. You must be a mind reader."

"What do you mean?" she asked, amazed at how calm she sounded.

"I've been trying to catch you all week," he said, reaching for her bag. "I wanted you to come to the cabin with me. Did Dan mention it?"

"No, in fact he didn't mention it when I called him this afternoon to make sure the cabin was clear." Now, *she* was gritting her teeth. She bent over Dorky, giving her head a gentle rub while wishing she could strangle dear, sweet, interfering Dan.

Pat looked at her quietly. "Let me guess. Everyone in our lives tried to talk about 'us' this week with you?"

Devon shot him a startled look. "You too?"

"Why do you think I wanted to come to the cabin? It was that or change my name and leave the state," he told her with a wry grin.

"Me too. I just needed time to think," she said softly.

He put her bag down and held out his arms. "Need a hug?"

She nodded as the tears started to fill her eyes.

"I am so confused," she said softly into his chest.

"I'm sorry, sweetheart." He held her, running his hands soothingly over her back. "I hate to see you hurting."

She nodded. "I know. I just needed some time to think."

He took a deep breath. "Do you want me to leave?"

Yes, her brain said. "No," her mouth uttered. If nothing else, perhaps this weekend would settle things. Either they were going to continue being friends, a thought that tore her heart a little more, or they were going to step into a completely new and terrifying territory. "Stay. Please," she asked.

Pat kissed her on the forehead. "Good girl," he said softly. He helped carry her things into the cabin. Pat started unloading the first bag of groceries in the kitchen. "Hmm," he said softly. "Fresh crab, breadsticks, real butter. Not good for the heart," he told her.

"But good for the soul," she murmured to herself.

"And all kinds of vegetable-looking stuff." He sighed as he pulled out the artichokes and avocados. "All your favorite foods," he said quietly, without looking at her. "You really have had a tough week. The only things missing are the chocolate-covered cherries."

She waved the box under his nose.

"I'm sorry," he said softly. "I didn't mean for . . ."

She covered his lips with her fingers. "Don't. No more apologies this weekend. Now, finish unloading before the best stuff melts."

Pat looked in the bag and grinned. "Quiche. I'm glad I already ate."

"Speaking of eating," Devon said. "Where is the kitten?"

"At home. Dan promised to feed it. The furball likes *him.*"

"How are you getting along?" she asked.

Pat sighed. "Fine, except every time I lay out my clothes in the morning, he rolls around on them and then gives me this smug look. I had to buy a new lint brush and I still haven't figured out how to keep him off my suits."

Devon choked back her laughter. "Good luck," she told him, amused by the grudging bond that Pat seemed to be developing with the kitten. "Have you thought of a name yet?"

"You mean Furball doesn't work for you?" he asked with a crooked grin.

"I don't think so. Although it works for somebody whose dog is named Dorky."

"Good point. All right. What would you name him?"

"Something elegant and noble."

Pat snorted in derision. "We are talking about the furball that flung cat litter all over my laundry room while he was digging to China?"

Devon laughed. "He won't always be a scruffy kitten. He will grow up to be a fat, arrogant kitty and then you'll be sorry you named him Muffin or Honey Bun."

Pat grimaced as he finished putting away the food. "Those names never crossed my mind," he assured her. "Terminator, Kamikaze, Tornado maybe."

Devon started rinsing the crabmeat while she remembered a similar conversation twenty years ago. "Do you remember helping me name Charlie?"

Pat moved behind her and began to rub her shoulders. "You wanted something noble then, as I remember."

"You said Charlemagne would be fitting and I could call him Charlie for short." She leaned back against his chest.

He looped his arms around her waist. "If I had only known," he said, kissing the top of her head. "The unconquered Charlie. I should have suggested something tame like Fluffy."

"It would never have fit." Devon turned in his arms. She looked into his gentle eyes and smiled. "Furball needs a good name too."

Pat kissed her cheeks, eyes and tip of her nose. "Ghengis Khan?"

"I don't think so," she told him, enjoying the playful nuzzling. "Ceasar, Zeus?"

"Alexander the Great?" he asked.

Their eyes locked. "Of course," she said. "We could call him Alex for short."

He shook his head. "Zander. Alex is too easy for Furball."

"Zander," she said, trying to picture the little ball of scruff grown up and cavorting through Pat's suit closet. "I like it."

Pat kissed her then. It was the most natural thing in the world, she decided, to be standing here kissing this wonderful man. It seemed all the pieces of the man that she loved were tied in this kiss. Sweet, strong, generous, and caring. Silly, intelligent, and creative. Devon sighed when he lifted his head. She rested her head on his shoulder. "Food. I need food."

"Hmm," he said, still holding her.

She tilted her head back and took a deep breath. "I love you."

His arms tightened around her as he smiled. "I love you, too." Then he gave her a wicked grin. "Ready to talk?"

"Nope."

He kissed her nose and turned her around. "Fix your dinner, Twerp," he said, using Dan's nickname for her when she was six. She shook her head as she heard him puttering with the small stereo. Soft Celtic music wafted through the cabin as she tried to focus on her dinner. She quickly made a salad, layered with crab, while Pat poured glasses of wine. He sat with her, eating a breadstick, asking her safe questions about the mansion renovation.

She suddenly remembered. "We found a secret room."

"Really?"

"It was probably an old storage closet but when it was remodeled fifty years ago, they sealed it up. I knew there was a dead space between the bedroom and stairs," she gloated. "The workers took out a section of wall and there it was."

"Any skeletons?"

She made a face. "No, better. There were some boxes. They had old children's clothes and toys and some books. Everything was in amazingly good condition. The interior designer went wild. It was a real find. She's already planning displays for all of it."

Pat watched Devon sparkle as she talked about her first love. The Rosemary mansion had been a passion of hers for years now and he was happy for her that her dreams were finally being realized. If not for her, the mansion would have been torn down to make room for an apartment building. Now, Eugene would have one of the most beautiful historical landmarks in the Northwest.

"What are you going to do when it's all finished?" he asked her.

She gave him a blank look. "What do you mean?"

"At the rate you're going, in a year it will be finished and open to the public."

She shrugged. "We still need to rebuild the carriage house and conservatory. There's a lot to be done." Her eyes twinkled. "And then there's the Grimsly house in Springfield. The owners are considering turning it into a parking lot. I suppose we'll try to convince them otherwise."

Pat laughed. "Heaven help them."

Feeling more at peace than she had in days, Devon washed her dishes and joined Pat in the cabin's small living room. While Dorky stretched out between them, Devon curled up on the couch with her papers from work and Pat did the same on the other couch. It wasn't long before her eyes struggled to stay open.

As Pat concentrated fiercely on some legal paperwork, a small line ran between his eyebrows. The day's growth of beard faintly shadowed his cheeks, giving him a darker, more intense look. He looked so serious, she thought tenderly, squelching the urge to stroke his cheek and see his eyes light up.

He looked up suddenly to catch her perusal. They sat for a moment, looking at each other as though for the first time.

Pat finally cleared his throat. "I'm going fishing in the morning. Want to come?"

Devon shook her head. "No, thank you. I think I'll just stay here and read."

He nodded and picked up his papers again. Then he glanced at her seriously. "Is there anything I can do for you?"

Love me, she thought. She shook her head softly. "Ask me that tomorrow," she told him. "If you dare," she teased.

Pat moved to sit beside her on the couch. Cupping a hand to her face, Pat tenderly told her, "You should know better than to dare me." Rubbing his thumb over her cheek he took a deep breath. "Promise me one thing?" he asked.

She nodded.

"Before we leave here, we'll talk. No matter what you have to say to me, it would be better than feeling like I'm losing you. This week was awful."

Devon clasped her hand over his and nodded, turning her cheek into his palm and letting his warmth and strength seep into her.

"I don't ever want to lose you," she admitted softly.

"You won't," he promised.

Devon knew he was right and no matter what his reaction to what she had to say, he would not turn away. The bond between them would have to be strong enough to survive this weekend. Devon lay her paperwork aside and, following her instincts, kissed him, a feather-like touch to his lips. They sat there, suspended together for a moment, then she pulled away.

"You need to get some sleep if you're going fishing," she told him and then, for some reason, ruffled his hair for a change. "I'll see you when you get back and before I leave, we'll talk."

She turned at the door to the bedroom. Pat was looking after her, some unreadable emotion giving him a pained expression. "Try not to drown, okay?" she asked.

"I promise."

She smiled. Pat always kept his promises.

Devon woke the next morning feeling disoriented. Where was she? A look toward her nightstand at home put her nose against a wall instead. She groaned and sat up, nearly hitting her head on the bunk bed. She was at the cabin, with Pat. Lying back on her pillow, she tried to form a coherent thought. It seemed she had spent most of the night tossing and turning and now she felt exhausted.

A glance at her watch showed six o'clock and she wondered if Pat had left yet. Trying not to trip in the dark, she crept down the hall and peered in his room. Dorky padded to her, nuzzling her hand softly. In the shadows, she could see Pat lay sleeping in the double bed. Funny, she couldn't remember ever watching him sleep before.

He lay on his back, one hand sprawled across the bed and one laying on his chest. He looked incredibly sexy as his tousled head turned to the side while he breathed in peaceful slumber. The covers had slid to his hips during the night, showing more than enough well-muscled, male chest to send her retreating to her room. Crawling back to her own bed, she pulled the covers up and carefully told herself a dozen reasons why she should lock the door. For his protection, not hers.

Dorky whined and nudged her. Telling herself she was under control and would not need that cold shower, she slipped out of bed. "All right girl. I get the hint," Devon said.

She opened the back door for the dog and took a deep breath of the mountain air. The first light was beginning to creep over the trees and the forest birds were just beginning to stir in the stillness. Even Dorky moved about quietly in the calm, morning peace.

Turning back, Devon ran into a solid body and nearly swallowed her heart.

"Sorry," Pat told her in a sleepy voice. "I heard something and forgot you were here."

"Gee, thanks," she told him dryly.

He rubbed a hand through his tousled hair. "I didn't mean that. I guess I didn't sleep very well last night."

"Join the club," she muttered.

"Hmm," he muttered in response. "Serves you right."

He looked tired and a bit dangerous with a heavy shadow on his cheeks. She was still in his arms, hands splayed on his chest as they stood in the darkened room.

Devon wondered if it was too late to take that cold shower.

"You should dress. It looks like it might rain," she told him helpfully.

Pat shrugged. "The way my luck has been going lately, I'm not surprised."

Then, without warning, he captured her in a bone-crushing embrace, and kissed her. His bare skin seemed on fire as her hands roamed over his chest. She ran her fingers in his hair, so soft and inviting and could feel his response to her as she struggled to get closer to him.

Pat buried his face in her hair and groaned, taking a deep breath. "Sorry. I've been wanting to do that for days." He let her go abruptly and walked away, closing the door to his room with a sharp click.

She barely had her coffee poured and her breathing under control when he reappeared, wearing jeans and a warm sweater. She stood paralyzed, wanting to say something but not sure what. In the awkward silence, he filled his thermos and picked up his coat. Turning at the door, he gave her a searching glance. Finally, sighing, he left the cabin, his footsteps softly thudding on the wooden steps.

Devon stayed in the kitchen, her heart aching, her stomach fluttering painfully. Now she knew what this feeling was and it had nothing to do with anything she ate. It was this incredible wanting that seemed to come from the very core of her being. An image of his face at the door tore a cry from her. It took a heartbeat to wrench open the door and run to the dock.

Pat looked up in surprise as she skidded to a stop on the bank. "Do you have an extra fishing pole?" she asked, wondering if she was losing her mind.

"I can get one," he said, a smile lighting his features.

Dorky barked madly and splashed in the water. "Is she coming with us?" Devon asked.

Pat sighed. "How can I leave her behind? She'd follow you to the ends of the earth." He put the poles in the boat. "You have that effect on dogs and people," he teased as he took her hand.

Devon stood suspended over the boat, one foot on the dock and one in the air. She glanced at Pat and for a moment they were kids again. Some devilment sparkled in his eyes and she shook her head. "You do and you're dead meat."

He grinned and steadied the boat with his foot. Devon sat down and tried to settle the wildly excited dog. She finally convinced Dorky to sit down and gave Pat a rueful grin. "I hear they mellow with age."

He started the boat motor and shook his head. "I hope not. I prefer insanely energetic to boring."

Devon wondered briefly if they were still talking about the dog.

They motored upstream to a wide spot in the river where the current slowed considerably and Pat dropped anchor before picking up his pole. "Want me to bait your line?" he asked.

Devon nodded and thought of the times Pat had quietly slipped something slimy on her hook before Dan noticed. Not that she hadn't had her share of worm flinging incidents with Dan. She took the line and cast it into the water, then sat quietly, rubbing Dorky's ear with her foot. Miraculously the dog settled on the bottom of the boat and lay her head over Devon's feet. Devon rewarded her with an occasional marshmallow from Pat's tackle box.

Pat became absorbed with his line and Devon took the opportunity to watch him. This scenario fit him perfectly, she thought. He was such a quiet, thoughtful man and yet underneath there swirled a greater intensity. That combination made him a gifted negotiator, able to see both sides of an issue and patient enough to see things to a satisfying conclusion.

It was why he loved his job with the city. He could be making a fortune in private practice but instead he doggedly worked on issues like parks and neighborhood rights. Known and respected as a fair arbitrator, many times he found an equitable solution where none seemed possible.

Pat reeled in another fish and gave her a delighted look as the trout flapped wildly about. Devon grinned at the boyish delight on his face and Dorky barked her approval as he stored the catch. "This is great weather for fishing," he said approvingly.

Devon gave the gray, gloomy sky a glance as Pat cast his line again. Only Pat would think this was great weather, she thought, inhaling the air that hung heavy with the scent of impending rain. The water fairies would have some job tonight, if the clouds blanketing the hills cut loose. She was as good a sport as the next woman about fishing, but sitting in a little boat in a driving rainstorm was where she drew the line. She forgot her reservations though, as something tugged her line. Carefully reeling it in, Devon tried to ignore her companions as Pat gave her advice and Dorky added a helpful bark to the process.

Pat grabbed the net and scooped up the fish, a good-sized trout. "It's a beauty," Pat congratulated her.

At that moment the threatening clouds chose to unload their cargo. With no warning, the rain beat down on them, pouring into the little boat as they scrambled to pull anchor and start the engine. Devon quickly stowed the gear, then wished for the rain slicker she had left hanging in the cabin. Apparently the water fairies decided the river needed a lot more water because it came down in buckets.

It only took a few minutes for them to reach the cabin, but in that time the three of them were soaked. Devon grabbed the fishing poles and gear, clamoring from the boat along with the dog. Pat tipped the engine up and covered it, then stowed the rest of the equipment. They raced to the cabin, then dumped the gear as they all shook like wet dogs under the cover of the old porch.

"Are you okay?" Pat asked.

"I'm f-f-fine," her teeth chattered while she stood there shaking.

"Go take a hot shower," Pat told her. "I'll clean the fish."

"You'll g-g-get s-s-soaked," Devon told him.

A drop of rain ran down his cheek as he smiled. "You think so?" he teased. He looked absolutely delighted to be standing in the cold mountain air, shivering and holding a line of fish. He also looked adorable. Good enough to offer to share a shower. In the interest of water conservation, she thought insanely as more rain pounded down around the cabin.

Fortunately her teeth were chattering too hard to make a valid proposition. It was just as well; she'd probably lose out to the fish anyway, she thought to herself. No, she decided, seeing the way Pat's eyes flared as he seemed to read her thoughts. She probably wouldn't lose out to the fish. She was the only one who seemed to have trouble making up her mind lately.

"Never mind," she sighed and tramped into the house.

Devon stripped her sodden clothes off and stepped into the steaming shower. Standing under the warm spray, she tried to get a grip on her raging emotions. This was one of those times when she wished she had Pat's clear logic. Okay, so what did she want? *Pat.*

That was easy, she thought in disgust. What was she afraid of? *Losing him completely.* The thought of life without him was unbearable but so was the thought of living in this emotional limbo of loving him but not having him.

She had always been the daring one, she reminded herself. Why was she so timid now? Because there was so much at stake. She shook her head. This uneasy wariness between them was driving her crazy. It felt like paddling toward a bend in the river and knowing there was something incredible just out of sight, yet worrying that it might be a hundred-foot waterfall. She toweled off and pulled on warm clothes, then started a fire in the fireplace. She could hear water running in the other bathroom. Then it stopped and Pat called for her.

"Devon, could you grab me a towel?" he called. She

retrieved a couple towels from the hall and walked in, turning her head discreetly as he reached for the towel. Suddenly a hand grabbed her and pulled her against a very wet, very male body. Pat laughed at her shocked expression, as he tried to hold a towel around his hips. "You looked too dry and comfortable. I thought I'd remedy that."

Taking a chance, she stayed in his arms. She cocked an eyebrow at him. "You should know better than to start something with me, Patrick Lawrence," she told him, entranced by the humor sparkling in his eyes.

"That's what I've been trying to do for weeks," he admitted, then kissed her soundly.

Devon stood in the bathroom gaping at him. "Oh," she squeaked.

He sighed. "Is this a good time to talk?"

She looked over his glistening body that still steamed from the shower and shook her head, trying to find her voice. "Not if you want me coherent," she admitted.

Surprise flared in his eyes. "I think I'd prefer you incoherent, sweetheart."

"Keep kissing me and it shouldn't be a problem," she told him, honestly.

"Is that a dare?" he asked in a husky voice.

She lay a hand on his cheek and rubbed the stubble there. "At this point, it's anything you want it to be," she whispered.

In response to her honesty, Pat buried his face in her

hair, holding her with one arm. "Good girl," he murmured. "That wasn't so hard was it?"

"You have no idea," she said, sounding incredibly put-upon. "When did I become such a goof?"

"I think that's one of those questions a defendant shouldn't answer."

"I love you," she said softly and walked out, leaving him standing there in the steam.

When Pat appeared, Devon was searching the kitchen for something to eat. She voted for quiche, but in the interest of their current truce, she thought something else might be more diplomatic.

Pat joined her, turning on the stove and reaching in the refrigerator for the plate of trout. "I'll cook, you get the table ready."

"You can cook for me anytime," she told him in the sultry voice Sunny had used here just a month ago. He gave her a wicked leer and captured her in an embrace. Another kiss and she forgot what she was hungry for. She leaned back in his arms, then sniffed. "Pat?"

"Hmm," he said, bending his head for another kiss.

"You're on fire."

"I know sweetheart," he groaned.

She pushed him away, batting at the smoldering edge of his T-shirt.

"Geez!" he shouted, swatting at the smoke with a towel. Then he gave her a disgusted look. "I know you make men burn, but this is ridiculous."

She turned him toward the dining table. "Why don't you set the table and try not to hurt yourself."

"Would you care?" he teased.

"More than you could imagine," she answered, kissing him lightly and shoving him from the kitchen.

The rain finally slowed to a light mist by the time they finished eating. Pat was being his most charming as they bantered back and forth, but Devon was starting to suffer from a severe case of nerves. Looking into his beautiful eyes, she felt as though the hundred-foot waterfall was rapidly approaching and soon it would be too late to turn her boat around. Pat looked at her in surprise as she reached for her hiking boots.

"I'm going for a walk," she said as he cleared the table.

"Do you want company?" he asked.

She held a hand out to him in answer. They walked along the river bank, hand in hand. Dorky trotted ahead, sniffing at every rock and tree. Devon found the spot she was looking for and sat on a log. The river bank widened, leaving a little canopied beach in the trees. It wasn't the first time she had come here.

"This was where I always came to get away from Dan," she told Pat.

"Even when you liked each other?" he asked.

She looked scandalized. "When was that?"

"College," he said quietly.

"Oh, then." Watching Pat try to look disinterested, she had to smile. Everyone else had asked about it and they usually were told to mind their own business.

"How come you never asked about it? Too polite?" she guessed.

"No, too scared," he told her, pitching pebbles into the river.

"What were you afraid of?" she asked in surprise.

"I guess I was afraid to know. That was the first summer I really noticed you." He looked at her. "You know. As more than just the kid I grew up with. I spent the summer trying to not make a pass at you and then you and Dan just seemed to hit it off. I guess I was afraid that was it. You two seemed perfect together."

Devon shook her head. She remembered how hard she had tried to avoid Pat that summer as well.

"It was no big deal," she told him, tossing a pebble into the river after his. "We went swimming at Slide Rock one afternoon."

His hand clenched hers at the mention of the rather famous make-out spot along the Willamette River. She slanted a look at him, noting the clenched jaw and tense look.

"It was beautiful and romantic and we kissed." She winced as his fingers flexed more tightly around hers. She sighed, deciding torturing Pat wasn't as much fun as torturing his baby brother. She squeezed his hand back. "It felt like kissing my brother."

He relaxed and nodded, silently mulling this, then his head snapped around. "Is that how you felt kissing me?" He sounded aghast.

"No," she told him. "Definitely not."

He looked inordinately pleased by that answer.

"Men," she muttered.

He grinned even more.

"Come on, before I push you in the river."

They walked back to the cabin, then stood on the porch looking at the river. Pulling her into his arms, Pat asked, "Want to talk?"

"No."

"Coward," he taunted. "I promise, it won't hurt."

She doubted that for a moment. Then she remembered being very young and confessing to Pat that she thought maybe a monster lived under her bed. He told her something she still lived by. It was better to face the monster and tell him to bug off, than waste her time being afraid. The monster peaked its head again and whispered that this thing she felt to the core of her being was something precious and she was treading on very dangerous ground. She silently told him to beat it. She was through listening to him.

She wrapped her arms around his waist and snuggled closer. "You're right," she whispered. "You could never hurt me."

Pat tilted her head back and faced her, nose to nose. "No, I never could." He looked into her eyes and sighed at whatever confusion he saw in her eyes. "Pushing you before you're ready is hurting you. I'm sorry." He kissed her forehead and stepped back. "I have some reports to finish. Mind if I work on them?"

She shook her head, feeling more strongly each moment as though she was avoiding something wonderful for fear of something that wasn't real, like the monster under the bed. She picked up her own work and sat on the couch next to Pat, then turned to curl her back against his shoulder. He lifted an arm to accommodate her and put a pillow under her head. The position was infinitely more comfortable and she wondered why they had never tried it before. *Because you've never been in love with each other before.* The possibility made her smile as she tried to concentrate on a carriage house floor plan.

"Comfy?" he asked the top of her head.

"Fine, how about you?" she asked, trying not to smile.

"I'll never get any work done," he admitted.

"I'll move," she offered innocently.

"No!"

"Good." Devon snuggled closer to his chest and started sketching the outside of the building.

After several attempts, she gave up, deciding while she may be comfortable, she was far too distracted to accomplish anything. Pat had been reading the same page himself for several minutes. She glanced up to see him looking at her, tenderness making his eyes soften to a warm golden color.

"Want to play something?" she asked.

He gave her a cautious smile.

"I meant backgammon," she quickly clarified.

"It wouldn't be my first choice," he admitted, but then he put away his briefcase and set up the board. Devon poured two cups of coffee and settled on the floor opposite him to play.

After three consecutive rolls of doubles, Pat gave her a disgusted look. "You are the luckiest person I know."

Devon thought of the way he looked at her earlier and had to silently agree with him. Of course, that sweet softness that enfolded her heart didn't stop her from trying to trounce him at the game. They played as they always had. She moved aggressively, knocking him out of the game, while he played defensively, making very few mistakes.

"You're just sore because this is the only game I have a chance of beating you," she told him after rolling another set of doubles.

He chuckled. "That's not true. You beat me at lots of things."

She snorted. "Golf, basketball, bowling? You always win. I could name a few dozen others." With a great deal of satisfaction she moved all of her markers off the board before he could even remove one. "Backgammon!"

He gave her an amused look. "I'm older. I'm supposed to beat you. Besides, you always beat me at odds and evens, even when you were little."

"Okay, loser fixes dinner and does the clean-up. Evens or odds?" she asked.

"Odds," he said, putting his fist out to count. "One, two, three! Darn it," he muttered.

"What are we eating?" she smugly asked.

"Hot dogs."

"Sorry, not while there is a perfectly good quiche in there."

Pat made gagging sounds and rolled on the floor, holding his throat. Devon giggled and couldn't resist. Pat had always been ticklish. She pounced on him, tickling him until he simply rolled her over and straddled her.

They both stopped laughing as this new thing between them pounded in their veins. "Want to talk?" Pat asked.

Devon arched an eyebrow. "Sure. Nice weather we're having."

He bent to kiss her, just enough to turn her brain to mush, then stood up and walked to the kitchen. "Just for that, you get hot dogs," he called back.

"Pat, I . . ." Devon followed him.

He put a finger over her lips. "I'm hungry and you're a coward. Let's eat."

She swatted his backside playfully as he stepped away, then took a step back at the look he gave her. "The river is mighty cold today," he warned, humor lightening the threat only a little.

"I didn't know you were such a poor loser," she told him.

"Yes you did. I hate to lose." He leaned down to whisper in her ear.

Devon tried to set the table without dropping anything. She apparently had never noticed what a pain in the tush the older Lawrence brother could be as well. She caught a glimpse of him behind the kitchen counter. Of course, with a tush like that, he could be a pain all he wanted, she thought.

She flushed as he caught her looking and grinned. Devon counted backward from a hundred and reminded herself that she could be a reasonable adult when the need arose. Throughout dinner she thought of the countless times she had been here with Pat. This place carried some of her happiest memories and most of them included this man. In recent years that had simply become a fact of life. She shared nearly everything in her life with him. Now it seemed they were about to share all of themselves and she realized that wasn't really what she was afraid of. She trusted him enough to know the future would be wonderful with him. She was mature enough to know that when things weren't wonderful, they would find a way to work through it. They had enough history to trust that this was real and healthy and absolutely what was meant to be.

What she feared was the moving on. She looked around the cabin and remembered the arguments over burnt marshmallows and who had caught more fish and who bluffed the best at poker. She remembered being little and jumping off the dock and knowing with absolute certainty that Pat would catch her. Those little girl memories were precious and she didn't ever want to lose them. She glanced at the man sitting on the floor watching her quietly and knew the future didn't mean leaving the past behind. It meant building on it and cherishing all that came before. In the future, other little girls would sit on that dock and ask their father where the water came from and he would tell them the wonderful story of the water fairies. She could feel her eyes filling with tears at the hope and promise of those future memories.

He looked concerned and she gave him a shaky smile. "I love you."

"Is that a good thing?"

"Yes," she said, nodding. "It's a wonderful thing." Devon kissed him on the cheek and said she needed fresh air. She walked to the dock and savored the serenity of this place. The skies had cleared just in time for the fading of the sun. The moon peeked over the mountains and it wouldn't be long before it was joined by endless, brilliant stars. Lying on the dock, she listened to the river bubble.

The dock squeaked as light footsteps came toward her. Pat sat down next to her. "How are you feeling?" she asked, still looking at the sky.

"Weird," he said quietly. "I've never thought twice about sitting with you on this dock. Now I don't know if you want me here or not."

She reached up a hand to his. He clasped it warmly and lay down next to her. Instinctively Devon rolled into his arms. She rested her head on his chest and laced her fingers with his.

"I don't know what I want anymore. I just know I don't want to lose you."

Pat's arms tightened about her as he kissed the top of her head. "I promise, sweetheart. No matter what, I'll always be here."

She tilted her face toward him. His face looked like

a timeless statue, carved from marble and perfectly proportioned in the fading light. He was as steady as marble, too, she thought, knowing that he would keep every promise he made to her, or kill himself trying. The heart beating under her cheek was made of something much finer than cold stone, though. It was a good heart, one that could grow and change with a lifetime of loving.

He ran a warm hand over her back. "I never wanted to hurt you. It seemed so simple at first." He chuckled. "Well, as simple as anything can be with you."

She pinched him, drawing another laugh.

"I just want to be with you," he said. "I thought for a long time that it was enough to just be friends but now, with this crazy curse, I don't know."

Devon bit her lip, her heart pounding. Then Pat shook his head. "No, that's a lie. I've known for a long time I wanted more, but I was the coward. I was too afraid to lose what we have by asking for more. Then, I thought I could convince you we belonged together but everything I did seemed to backfire and push you away." She could see the corners of his mouth lift in the shadows. He turned to look at her, longing and so much emotion in his eyes that her throat tightened. "I love you. I will love you for the rest of my days. What we have didn't just happen. It's been growing for years. We're just finally starting to realize it."

She reached her fingers to his mouth, touching the softness there. "I love you, too. I'm terrified of what's happening between us, but I can't stop it. I don't want to stop it," she told him.

Pat kissed her then, softly savoring her lips, molding her to him. Devon responded with all her heart, touching her tongue to his, finally enjoying what she had been denying for too long.

When Pat pulled away to look at her, she saw all the love she could want in his eyes. "I love you, Patrick Michael Lawrence. I will love you for the rest of my life," she told him. He rewarded her with a kiss that stole her breath and her mind.

Lying in his arms, as the river rushed headily by, Devon wondered if the water fairies would be pleased. Yes, she thought. Any boy who would tell their tale to a little girl would definitely win their approval. The fairies could rest assured the lovely man holding her would continue to tell the story to his daughters and their daughters. She thought she saw a flash of silver on the water but it may have been the joy that seemed to fill her throat and her eyes.

Chapter Fourteen

Pat parked in front of Devon's parents' house and took a deep breath. This was the house he had been welcome in for thirty-four years, he reminded himself. Of course, that was before he fell in love with their daughter.

Devon gave him a curious look. "Everything okay?"

"Fine," he lied. She was naively unaware that he was about to change his life and his relationship with her parents forever. Especially his relationship with her father. Pat wiped his sweating palms on his slacks. He tried to remind himself this man was like a second father to him. Michael Kelly had mentored him through his law career. He had taught Pat how to fly fish. He had given him advice on not pulverizing Dan over the years.

Hang 'em high Kelly. Pat started seeing spots before his eyes.

Devon winced and pried his fingers off hers. "I don't think when they invited us to dinner that they meant to have *us* as the main course," she told him helpfully.

Pat gave her a befuddled look.

"That was a joke," she told him dryly. Devon shook her head. Pat had been calmer before his first big court case than he seemed facing her parents today.

Her mother opened the door and smiled broadly for them. "Devon, come on in. Since when do you ring the door, you two?" Devon's mother gave them both a wide-eyed, innocent look.

Devon hugged her and whispered, "Tell that to Pat." The two women shared an amused look as Pat stood uncomfortably in the foyer.

Maggie Kelly gave him a quick hug. "We haven't seen you in weeks, Pat. How have you been?"

"Fine, thank you," he told her.

Maggie shot her daughter a questioning look at Pat's polite, albeit worried expression and Devon shrugged. Devon pulled Pat into the living room where her father waited.

"Devi!" her father boomed. Michael Kelly was a big man, the grandson of Irish immigrants, and his voice reverberated through the house the same way it filled a courtroom. "How's my little girl?" he asked, giving her a bone-crushing embrace.

"Fine, Daddy. How have you been? I saw you on the news with the Sullivan case."

Her father shook his head sadly. "Terrible business

that. Any man who marries a fine woman and treats her that badly should be shot." He gave Pat an odd look. "Are you all right, son? You look a bit pale. They're not working you too hard at city hall, are they?"

"No," Pat answered. "I just haven't been getting enough sleep lately." Devon's father arched an eyebrow nearly to his hairline and Pat blushed scarlet as he wondered if he'd implied something he hadn't meant to. He looked to Devon for help. She arched a disbelieving eyebrow at him and shook her head in disgust.

"I'm not sure I agree with you about Sullivan," she told her father, trying to change the subject before Pat stepped any deeper in the mire.

"You think what he did to his wife was all right?" Michael asked his daughter.

"Which one?" Devon asked. "I mean they all thought he was their husband. Just because one got him first."

"Well, in the eyes of the law, the first one was his only true wife. Though the others had every right to want him strung up on chicken wire, too," her father admitted.

"But that was just it. At the sentencing, they all testified for him. They said they'd rather share him than have him sent to prison."

Michael snorted and turned to Pat. "Can you explain that to me? Wouldn't you think a man like that should be punished?"

Pat nodded as her father pinned him with that famous, "Kelly sentencing stare." "Yes, sir," he said, audibly swallowing.

"Michael," Maggie Kelly admonished her husband

softly. Devon wondered at the look of devilment in her father's eyes.

Michael wagged a finger at Pat and boldly continued. "If those women were my daughters, I'd have been the first one in line to see him punished. Made me wish firing squads weren't outlawed."

Pat sank weakly onto the couch next to Devon, then scooted to the opposite end as Devon noticed he was losing more color by the minute. She gave her mother a beseeching look. Thankfully the doorbell rang. Maggie gave her husband one more warning look before leaving to answer the door.

"Well, hello. Come on in." Devon heard her mother's greeting, then glanced at Pat in surprise as his own parents walked into the room.

"Robert, good to see you." Michael shook his best friend's hand. "Since we never see you kids anymore, we thought we might as well all get together at once," he explained to Devon.

Devon shot a worried look at Pat as he hugged his mother. Alicia Lawrence patted her son's cheek and whispered something that drew a shaky smile from him.

Before Devon's father could start in on any more questionable topics, Maggie announced dinner was ready. Devon helped her mother serve as Pat sat down, looking for all the world like a condemned man at his last meal.

"Is Margaret back yet?" Pat's mother asked politely about his assistant.

"Yes, she returned Monday," Pat told her. "She said

she had the time of her life. She's already making plans to see her other grandkids in California." Pat shook his head. "She has so much vacation time still saved, I may never see her again."

"Vacation," Michael Kelly said. "I think I have some vacation time coming myself."

"We should go fishing," Pat's father said. "That is, if we can use the cabin. Seems like you youngsters are using it all the time now. How has the fishing been this summer?"

"Pat made his biggest catch ever this summer," Devon quipped.

Pat sent her a look promising retribution, but she was starting to enjoy his discomfort just the tiniest bit. Funny, how she had always thought Pat unflappable, but this evening seemed to be unraveling his calm more with each passing moment. It was good for him though, she told herself. It was always a good idea to keep him from getting too stuffy.

"I can't say as I blame you for using the cabin so often," her mother told Pat. "What with all this McKenzie Man nonsense, I'm surprised you haven't just moved to the cabin permanently."

Pat shot Devon a smug look as she wondered exactly whose side her mother was on.

"I don't think it's nonsense," Devon said. "I think the curse is kind of sweet."

Her father snorted. "Sweet if you're a female barracuda. Can't say as I blame Pat either for hiding out at the cabin. I wouldn't want to be saddled with a woman for the rest of my life just because of some curse nonsense. A man needs to take his time, find the right kind of girl. Someone who is sweet and loving, who'll be a dutiful wife and know her place."

Pat looked from Devon whose chin was nearly on the table to her mother who looked like she might sweetly throw something at her beloved and tried not to laugh. His own mother was carefully studying the flower arrangement on the table while his father shared an amused look with Devon's father. Somehow none of this was going quite the way he planned it. Was it too late to simply plea bargain his way out of this?

He spent the next two hours trying to find some excuse to talk to Devon's father privately. After dinner the older adults took exceptional interest in Devon's plans for the Rosemary mansion. Then they asked him countless questions about the city's efforts to renovate one of the downtown parks. Finally, Michael mentioned some legal case that might be helpful to him and went to his office to find the reference. Pat practically bolted after him, shutting the door and then wondering what he was going to say.

"Could I have a word with you?" he started.

Devon's father interrupted. "Good to see you settle that youth center business. Moving the police department's school safety program to the same building was a perfect solution. The kids have supervision and the businesses feel safe with all the police uniforms around. You did a fine job on that one."

"Judge, I want to ask you," Pat began, squaring his shoulders and taking a deep breath. "I—"

"Ask away, son. You know I consider you a son. I'm darned proud of you, even if my daughter chose not to follow in the family business," Michael Kelly said with a heavy sigh. "I do love her even though she is a willful young woman." Devon's father shook his head. "I don't envy the man she decides to settle down with. I think he should have a strong constitution."

Pat shifted on his feet again and nodded in agreement, "That's true, but I—"

The judge cut him off, "Not that I'm saying she's not worth it. She would make a great partner, a woman a man could really count on. She has a good head on her shoulders and she doesn't buckle under when things get tough."

"No sir," Pat tried again.

"But stubborn," the older man continued, turning to the window, his voice oddly strained. "I don't believe I have ever seen a woman with such a stubborn streak, except her mother," he acknowledged. "But a quick mind, she's a great one for debate if you can get a word in edgewise."

"She's not the only one," Pat muttered, wondering how he had completely lost control of his life.

"Excuse me?" Devon's father turned to him.

"I mean . . ." Pat flushed. "Judge, if I could finish, I know she's your daughter and believe me, I know all of her personality flaws."

At the imperious look on Michael Kelly's face, Pat

shook his head ruefully. This wasn't going well. He tried again. "I just want you to know that I know Devon probably better than anyone." He flushed as the older man's eyebrow arched. "I mean—oh man, I don't know what I mean."

He sank down on the leather chair across from the desk. "I'm in love with Devon. I know it seems crazy and I know this seems sudden, but I love her with all my heart and will spend the rest of my life loving her."

He looked up at the older man and stopped talking. Devon's father turned back to the window, bent over, his shoulders shaking.

"Judge! Oh geez. I shouldn't have sprung this on you. I should have given you time. I know this is really a shock."

Pat rushed to the older man as he wondered if Michael had a weak heart that he didn't know about. For a fleeting moment, he wondered how Devon's father could have a weak heart and survive twenty-eight years with his daughter.

While Pat debated calling 911, he helped the older man straighten. As the judge stood up, Pat saw him wiping tears of laughter from his eyes as he tried to catch a breath between bouts of hilarity.

"Oh, ho! Pat, my boy, I didn't think I would ever see the day when you'd stand before me tongue-tied and falling apart at the seams. I guess I should have known it would be over Devi." He embraced Pat in a bear hug and laughed again. "Son, if you think twenty-eight years is too sudden for you two nitwits to realize you were made for each other, I hate to think how long it's going to take for me to have grandchildren."

Pat stood flabbergasted as Michael sat at his desk and pulled a cigar out of his desk drawer. A discreet knock at the door preceded Pat's father sticking his head in. "May I?"

Pat watched the two old friends share a knowing, amused look and wondered if this jury had been rigged from the start.

"Oh, by all means," Michael announced. "You should enjoy this, too." Devon's father warmed to the prospect. "Your firstborn was just explaining to me how he is going to do right by my baby." He narrowed his most ferocious sentencing look upon Pat. "At least, I hope that's what all this stammering is about."

Pat looked from one man to the other and sat back. "Maybe I should reconsider my defense," he answered dryly.

The judge laughed. "Too late, son. I sentence you to a lifetime of bailing your wife out of whatever crazy mess she's jumped into."

The two older men were equally enjoying this as Pat grinned in agreement.

"And I thought you wanted me to be a lawyer to pass on your knowledge. You just needed free legal advice for your daughter," he said.

The two older man guffawed as Michael handed cigars all around. Pat smelled the cigar and looked at the two men he loved so dearly. He knew by their delighted expressions that they looked forward to a future for their children that would never be dull. He clipped the end of the cigar and had to admit, it was exactly the future he wanted.

Chapter Fifteen

"Where did this summer go?" Leslie sighed as she lay back on the lounge chair. The sounds of children splashing in Pat's pool mixed with adults laughing and enjoying each other's company. Pat had invited his family, Devon's parents, and some close friends for a barbecue, taking advantage of the remaining days of summer. Devon also wondered if it was his way of letting everyone know their relationship had changed. Although from the amused looks they had received, she gathered it wasn't exactly a secret. Devon knew absolutely that Pat had ulterior motives for inviting the woman talking to her mother. It had been with a great deal of relief that they had agreed the *McKenzie Magazine's* publisher should come to the party.

"Have you ever noticed how strangely the men act around Eugenia Barstow?" Leslie asked her.

Devon had to laugh as Mitch dove into the pool to avoid Eugenia, unfortunately forgetting to remove his shirt first.

"She does know how to make an appearance," Devon said, shaking her head.

Eugenia looked stunning in a flowing summer dress, diamonds sparkling at her ears and neck. The woman stood out in any crowd, but here she created chaos with the single men around. As Eugenia mingled, they acted like magnets pushed by an opposing force, scooting to the opposite side of the yard, and then to the house when she came within sight. Except Pat of course. He was delighted to have the woman present, had even greeted Devon with a sizzling kiss in front of her.

What a difference a few weeks could make, Devon thought, relaxing in the shade, stroking Zander. A month ago she sat in this chair watching Pat and wondering what the future held for them. Now, she watched him wrestling the meat tongs from Dan at the barbecue and knew no matter what the future held, they would be together. He glanced up to see her watching and waved. She waved back just as Tyler blasted him with a squirt gun. The child shrieked and tore across the yard with Pat in hot pursuit. Watching Pat still made Devon's heart ache, but now it was a good feeling. He was hers—always had been, always would be.

Pat finally caught Tyler and held him by his ankles

over the pool while the boy giggled and taunted him, hoping he would let go. Pat swung the boy right-side-up and gently tossed him in the water near his father. The child came up laughing. "Can we do it again?"

Pat walked toward Devon, laughter still lighting his face. He bent to kiss her soundly, then sat on the edge of the lounge chair. "How are you two?"

"Fine," Devon told him, stroking his cheek.

Leslie stood up and gave them an amused look. "I think I'll get a veggie burger before your brother burns them all."

"You're letting Dan cook?" Devon asked as Leslie walked away.

Pat nodded. "I had more important things to do." He bent and kissed her again, this time taking his time.

When he finally lifted his head Devon was breathless. "Definitely more important things," she told him, then drew him back for more.

After several moments of feeling oblivious to their surroundings or even a need for oxygen, Pat pulled away. He gave her a brisk look. "Actually I came over to ask for help."

"You don't need any, you're doing fine," she teased, rubbing her thumb over his lips.

He gave her a wicked grin. "Thank you, sweetheart, but I meant in the house. I need help carrying some more drinks up from the basement."

Devon frowned. "Why are the drinks down there?"

"I put in a new refrigerator," he said, taking her hand.

"Does this mean I'm to be allowed in the basement?"

she asked with great drama. Pat had expressly forbidden her from going down there in the past couple of weeks. Unfortunately he knew her well enough that he had also gone to great lengths not to leave her alone in the house, knowing perfectly well her curiosity would get the better of her.

Pat stopped and slapped his forehead. "I forgot."

"Too late," she told him gleefully. "You already told me I had to help you."

He gave her a serious look. "Okay, but you have to keep your eyes closed."

Devon rolled her eyes. "That should be easy, walking through a basement I haven't been in for weeks, looking for a refrigerator I've never seen, and keeping my eyes closed. I do love you," she told him.

He stopped at the top of the basement stairs. Giving her a look so serious that it nearly stopped her heart, he kissed her again. "I love you, too. More than life." Then he grinned. "Close your eyes."

She covered her eyes with one hand while he led her down the stairs, holding the other. At the bottom step he warned her, "No peeking."

"Spoil sport," she muttered as he led her around the room. Even sneaking the tiniest peek, she couldn't see anything. The basement was dark, lit only by the small windows high on the wall. Then a light came on and he told her, "Okay, you can look."

Devon opened her eyes and started to tease him about his secrecy, then stopped. There before her was the train. He had built a U-shaped table with three times the track of his previous layout. The mountains needed paint and it would take weeks to make enough trees for it, but it was beautiful. Pat flipped a switch and the train started puffing around the track.

"You built a tunnel," she whispered. She walked in the center of the design and looked through the little town that he had painstakingly repaired. The tiny, Victorian buildings stood against a backdrop of mountains that would be wonderful when everything was finished.

It still needed a lot of work, but the foundation was solid, Devon thought, running a finger over one tiny roofline. That was the most important thing, in trains and relationships, she decided as she saw the changes he had added. This foundation was perfect.

"Oh, Pat, it's wonderful. I love it."

"Really," he said thoughtfully. "You haven't seen the best part."

"There's more?"

"Since I had more track, I thought I'd add a few more cars." He pointed to the train puffing to her. "I really like the yellow freight car myself."

She watched the train puff by and thought it did look nice now that it was longer. "I still like the caboose best," she told him as it rounded the corner and headed for the tunnel again.

Pat gave her an amused look. "I think you'll like the new freight cars better though."

As she watched the train chug along, she noticed something sitting in the open bed of the yellow car. Waiting impatiently for the train to reappear from the tunnel, she stole a glance at Pat. His expression was so tender she had to swallow back the lump in her throat. The train finally pulled to a stop in front of her and she stood frozen, staring at the jeweler's box nestled in the cotton bedding.

"Go ahead, sweetheart. Open it," Pat's soft voice caressed her.

With shaking fingers, Devon picked up the box and stared at it, her mind a complete blank. She felt Pat take the box from her and flip open the lid. Inside, a perfect diamond winked at her, set in delicate, rose filigree. The old-fashioned setting was elegant and beautiful, yet the striking diamond captured her attention as it flashed bits of rainbow light about the room. If she could have designed the perfect ring, this would be it. A tear trickled down her cheek as she simply stood there, unable to move.

"If you don't like it, we'll get you another one. You can pick out any setting you want, Devi," Pat told her, panic creeping into his voice. "If you don't want diamonds, you can have something else. I don't care as long as you're happy," he told her, snapping the box shut and putting it back in the train car.

Devon shook her head and more tears flowed down her cheeks. She reached for the box and took a deep, shaky breath. "It's the most beautiful thing I've ever seen," she told him. Relief lit his features as he slipped the ring on her finger. "It's perfect for me," she told him. "Just like you."

Pat pulled her into his arms for a fierce kiss, giving

her all of his passion and strength. "I love you," he whispered in her ear as he ran kisses over her damp cheeks. "I love you so much."

Devon lay her cheek against his and savored the moment, then a thought made her giggle. "I think I know the first person you want to see this."

Pat gave her a rueful grin. "The sooner, the better."

She took his hand. "Let's go find Eugenia."

"She was trying to find Dan the last I saw her," Pat told her, his voice heavy with amusement.

"Heaven help the ladies," Devon murmured.

"Heaven help my baby brother," he corrected.

Hand in hand they walked up the stairs toward the sounds of laughter and love.